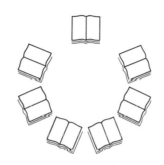

The Junior Great Books Reading and Discussion Program

JUNIOR GREAT BOOKS

SERIES 4

VOLUME ONE

A Program of Interpretive Reading and Discussion

The Great Books Foundation
a nonprofit educational corporation

Published and distributed by
The Great Books Foundation
a nonprofit educational corporation
40 East Huron Street
Chicago, Illinois 60611

Acknowledgments

All possible care has been taken to trace ownership and secure permission for each selection in this series. The Great Books Foundation wishes to thank the following authors, publishers, and representatives for permission to reprint copyright material:

The Emperor's New Clothes from IT'S PERFECTLY TRUE AND OTHER STORIES translated by Paul Leyssac. Copyright © 1938 by Paul Leyssac, renewed 1966 by Mary Rehan. Reprinted by permission of Harcourt Brace Jovanovich, Inc.

Allah Will Provide from THE SULTAN'S FOOL AND OTHER NORTH AFRICAN TALES by Robert Gilstrap and Irene Estabrook. Copyright © 1958 by Robert Gilstrap and Irene Estabrook.

Vasilissa the Beautiful from RUSSIAN WONDER TALES by Post Wheeler. Copyright © 1912 by The Century Co. Revised edition copyright 1946 by Post Wheeler. By permission of A. S. Barnes & Company, Inc.

The Story of Dr. Dolittle from THE STORY OF DR. DOLITTLE by Hugh Lofting. Copyright © 1920 by Hugh Lofting, renewed 1948 by Josephine Lofting. By permission of Christopher Lofting.

Prince Rabbit from PRINCE RABBIT AND THE PRINCESS WHO COULD NOT LAUGH by A. A. Milne. Copyright © 1966 by Dorothy Daphne Milne and Spencer Curtis Brown. By permission of Curtis Brown, Ltd.

The Imp in the Basket from THE DEVIL'S STORYBOOK by Natalie Babbitt. Copyright © 1974 by Natalie Babbitt. Reprinted by permission of Farrar, Straus & Giroux, Inc.

The Goldfish from THE LITTLE BOOKROOM by Eleanor Farjeon. Copyright © 1955 by Eleanor Farjeon. Reprinted by permission of Harold Ober Associates, Inc.

Ali Baba and the Forty Thieves translated by Charlotte Dixon, from TALES FROM THE ARABIAN NIGHTS edited by Dr. Hedwig Smola. Copyright © 1964 by Verlag Carl Ueberreuter, Vienna, Austria. By permission of Verlag Carl Ueberreuter.

Illustration Credits

Natalie Babbitt's illustration for *The Imp in the Basket* is from THE DEVIL'S STORYBOOK by Natalie Babbitt. Copyright © 1974 by Natalie Babbitt. Reprinted by permission of Farrar, Straus & Giroux, Inc.

Brock Cole prepared the illustrations for this edition of *The Red Balloon* and *Allah Will Provide*.

Donna Diamond prepared the illustration for this edition of *Vasilissa the Beautiful*.

Leo and Diane Dillon prepared the illustration for this edition of *The Goldfish*.

Rudyard Kipling's illustration for *The Elephant's Child* is from JUST SO STORIES by Rudyard Kipling. Published by Schocken Books, Inc.

Hugh Lofting's illustration for *The Story of Dr. Dolittle* is from THE STORY OF DR. DOLITTLE. Copyright © 1920 by Hugh Lofting, renewed 1948 by Josephine Lofting. By permission of Christopher Lofting.

W. B. Park prepared the illustration for this edition of *Prince Rabbit*.

Arthur Rackham's illustrations for *The Emperor's New Clothes* and *Ali Baba and the Forty Thieves* are from THE ARTHUR RACKHAM FAIRY BOOK. Reprinted by permission of Harrap Ltd.

Charles Robinson's illustration for *The Devoted Friend* is from THE HAPPY PRINCE AND OTHER TALES by Oscar Wilde. Published by Shambhala Publications, Inc.

Ernest H. Shepard's illustration for *Mr. Toad* is from THE WIND IN THE WILLOWS by Kenneth Grahame. Copyright © 1933 by Charles Scribner's Sons, renewed 1961 by Ernest H. Shepard. Reprinted with the permission of Charles Scribner's Sons.

Cover illustrations by Pamela Noftsinger, Leo and Diane Dillon, and Brock Cole.

Cover and book design by Michael Waitsman and Liane Sebastian, Synthesis Concepts, Inc.

contents

The Red Balloon

Albert Lamorisse

Once upon a time in Paris there lived a little boy whose name was Pascal. He had no brothers or sisters, and he was very sad and lonely at home.

Once he brought home a lost cat, and some time later a stray puppy. But his mother said animals brought dirt into the house, and so Pascal was soon alone again in his mother's clean well-kept rooms.

Then one day, on his way to school, he caught sight of a fine red balloon, tied to a street lamp. Pascal laid his schoolbag on the ground. He climbed up the lamppost, untied the balloon, and ran off with it to the bus stop.

But the conductor knew the rules. "No dogs," he said. "No large packages, no balloons."

People with dogs walk.

People with packages take taxis.

1

People with balloons leave them behind.

Pascal did not want to leave his balloon behind, so the conductor rang the signal bell and the bus went on without him.

Pascal's school was a long way off, and when he finally reached the school door it was already shut. To be late for school and with a balloon—that was unheard of! Pascal was very worried.

Then he had an idea. He left his balloon with the janitor, who was sweeping the yard. And since it was the first time that he had ever been late, he was not punished.

When school was over, the janitor, who had kept the balloon in his room for Pascal, gave it back to him.

But it had begun to rain. And Pascal had to walk home because of those silly rules about balloons on buses. But he thought his balloon shouldn't get wet.

There was an old gentleman just going by, and Pascal asked him whether he and the balloon could take shelter under his umbrella. So, from one umbrella to another, Pascal made his way home.

His mother was glad to see him finally come home. But since she had been very worried, she was angry when she found out that it was a balloon that had made Pascal late. She took the balloon, opened the window, and threw it out.

Now, usually when you let a balloon go, it flies away. But Pascal's balloon stayed outside the window, and the two of them looked at each other through the glass. Pascal was surprised that his balloon hadn't flown away, but not really as surprised as all that. Friends will do all kinds of things for you. If the friend happens to be a

2

balloon, it doesn't fly away. So Pascal opened his window quietly, took his balloon back inside, and hid it in his room.

The next day, before he left for school, Pascal opened the window to let his balloon out and told it to come to him when he called.

Then he picked up his schoolbag, kissed his mother good-bye, and went downstairs.

When he reached the street he called: "Balloon! Balloon!" and the balloon came flying down to him.

Then it began to follow Pascal—without being led by a string, just as if it were a dog following its master.

But, like a dog, it didn't always do as it was told. When Pascal tried to catch it to cross the street, the balloon flew beyond his reach.

Pascal decided to pretend he didn't care. He walked up the street just as if the balloon weren't there at all and hid behind the corner of a house. The balloon got worried and hurried to catch up with him.

When they got to the bus stop, Pascal said to the balloon: "Now, balloon, you follow me. Don't lose sight of the bus!"

That was how the strangest sight came to be seen in a Paris street—a balloon flying along behind a bus.

When they reached Pascal's school, the balloon again tried not to let itself be caught. But the bell was already ringing and the door was just about to close, so Pascal had to hurry in alone. He was very worried.

But the balloon flew over the school wall and got in line behind the children. The teacher was very surprised to see this strange new pupil, and when the balloon tried to follow them into the classroom, the children made so much noise that the principal came along to see what was happening.

The principal tried to catch the balloon to put it out the door. But he couldn't. So he took Pascal by the hand and marched him out of school. The balloon left the classroom and followed them.

The principal had urgent business at the Town Hall, and he didn't know what to do with Pascal and his balloon. So he locked the boy up inside his office. The balloon, he said to himself, would stay outside the door.

But that wasn't the balloon's idea at all. When it saw that the principal had put the key in his pocket, it sailed along behind him as he walked down the street.

All the people knew the principal very well, and when they saw him walking past followed by a balloon they shook their heads and said: "The principal's playing a joke. It isn't right; a principal should be dignified, he shouldn't be playing like one of the boys in his school."

The poor man tried very hard to catch the balloon, but he couldn't, so there was nothing for him to do but put up with it. Outside the Town Hall the balloon stopped. It waited for him in the street, and when the principal went back to school the balloon was still behind him.

The principal was only too glad to let Pascal out of his office and to be rid of him and his balloon.

On the way home Pascal stopped to look at a picture in a sidewalk exhibit. It showed a little girl with a hoop. Pascal thought how nice it would be to have a friend like that little girl.

But just at that moment he met a real little girl, looking just like the one in the picture. She was wearing a pretty white dress, and she held in her hand the string . . . to a blue balloon!

Pascal wanted to be sure she noticed that his balloon was a magic one. But his balloon wouldn't be caught, and the little girl began to laugh.

Pascal was angry. "What's the use of having a trained balloon if it won't do what you want?" he said to himself. At that very moment some of the tough boys of the neighborhood came by. They tried to catch the balloon as it trailed along behind Pascal. But the balloon saw the danger. It flew to Pascal at once. He caught it and began to run, but more boys came to corner him from the other side.

So Pascal let go of his balloon, which immediately rose high into the sky. While the boys were all looking up, Pascal ran between them to the top of the steps. From there he called his balloon, which came to him at once—to the great surprise of the boys in the gang.

So Pascal and his balloon got home without being caught.

The next day was Sunday. Before he left for church, Pascal told his balloon to stay quietly at home, not to break anything, and especially not to go out. But the balloon did exactly as it pleased. Pascal and his mother were hardly seated in church when the balloon appeared and hung quietly in the air behind them.

Now, a church is no place for a balloon. Everyone was looking at it and no one was paying attention to the service. Pascal had to leave in a hurry, followed out by the church guard. His balloon certainly had no sense of what was proper. Pascal had plenty of worries!

All this worry had made him hungry. And as he still

had his coin for the collection plate, he went into a bakeshop for some cake. Before he went inside he said to the balloon: "Now be good and wait for me. Don't go away."

The balloon was good, and only went as far as the corner of the shop to warm itself in the sun. But that was already too far. For the gang of boys who had tried to catch it the day before saw it, and they thought that this was the moment to try again. Without being seen they crept up to it, jumped on it, and carried it away.

When Pascal came out of the bakeshop, there was no balloon! He ran in every direction, looking up at the sky. The balloon had disobeyed him again! It had gone off by itself! And although he called at the top of his voice, the balloon did not come back.

The gang had tied the balloon to a strong string, and they were trying to teach it tricks. "We could show this magic balloon in a circus," one of them said. He shook a stick at the balloon. "Come here or I'll burst you," he shouted.

As luck would have it, Pascal saw the balloon over the top of a wall, desperately dragging at the end of its heavy string. He called to it.

As soon as it heard his voice, the balloon flew toward him. Pascal quickly untied the string and ran off with his balloon as fast as he could run.

The boys raced after them. They made so much noise that everyone in the neighborhood stopped to watch the chase. It seemed as if Pascal had stolen the boys' balloon. Pascal thought: "I'll hide in the crowd." But a red balloon can be seen anywhere, even in a crowd.

Pascal ran through narrow alleys, trying to lose the gang of boys.

At one point the boys didn't know whether Pascal had turned right or left, so they split up into several groups. For a minute Pascal thought he had escaped them, and he looked around for a place to rest. But as he rounded a corner he bumped right into one of the gang. He ran back the way he had come, but there were more boys there. He was desperate—he ran up a side street which led to an empty lot. He thought he'd be safe there.

But suddenly boys appeared from every direction, and Pascal was surrounded.

So he let go of his balloon. But this time, instead of chasing the balloon, the gang attacked Pascal. The balloon flew a little way off, but when it saw Pascal fighting it came back. The boys began throwing stones at the balloon.

"Fly away, balloon! Fly away!" Pascal cried. But the balloon would not leave its friend.

Then one of the stones hit the balloon, and it burst.

While Pascal was crying over his dead balloon, the strangest thing happened!

Everywhere balloons could be seen flying up into the air and forming a line high into the sky.

It was the revolt of all captive balloons!

And all the balloons of Paris came down to Pascal, dancing around him, twisting their strings into one strong one and lifting him up into the sky. And that was how Pascal took a wonderful trip all around the world.

The Emperor's New Clothes

Hans Christian Andersen

Many years ago there lived an Emperor who was so
exceedingly fond of fine new clothes that he spent all
his money on being elaborately dressed. He took no
interest in his soldiers, no interest in the theater, nor
did he care to drive about in his state coach, unless it
were to show off his new clothes. He had different robes
for every hour of the day, and just as one says of a King
that he is in his Council Chamber, people always said of
him, "The Emperor is in his wardrobe!"

The great city in which he lived was full of gaiety.
Strangers were always coming and going. One day two
swindlers arrived. They made themselves out to be
weavers and said they knew how to weave the most
magnificent fabric that one could imagine. Not only
were the colors and patterns unusually beautiful, but
the clothes that were made of this material had the

extraordinary quality of becoming invisible to everyone who was either unfit for his post or inexcusably stupid.

"What useful clothes to have!" thought the Emperor. "If I had some like that, I might find out which of the people in my Empire are unfit for their posts. I should also be able to distinguish the wise from the fools. Yes, that material must be woven for me immediately!" Then he gave the swindlers large sums of money so that they could start work at once.

Quickly they set up two looms and pretended to weave, but there was no trace of anything on the frames. They made no bones about demanding the finest silk and the purest gold thread. They stuffed everything into their bags and continued to work at the empty looms until late into the night.

"I'm rather anxious to know how much of the material is finished," thought the Emperor, but to tell the truth, he felt a bit uneasy, remembering that anyone who was either a fool or unfit for his post would never be able to see it. He rather imagined that he need not have any fear for himself, yet he thought it wise to send someone else first to see how things were going. Everyone in the town knew about the exceptional powers of the material, and all were eager to know how incompetent or how stupid their neighbors might be.

"I will send my honest old Chamberlain to the weavers," thought the Emperor. "He will be able to judge the fabric better than anyone else, for he has brains, and nobody fills his post better than he does."

So the nice old Chamberlain went into the hall where the two swindlers were sitting working at the empty looms.

"Upon my life!" he thought, opening his eyes very wide, "I can't see anything at all!" But he didn't say so.

Both the swindlers begged him to be good enough to come nearer, and asked how he liked the unusual design and the splendid colors. They pointed to the empty looms, and the poor old Chamberlain opened his eyes wider and wider, but he could see nothing, for there was nothing. "Heaven above!" he thought, "could it possibly be that I am stupid? I have never thought that of myself, and not a soul must know it. Could it be that I am not fit for my post? It will never do for me to admit that I can't see the material!"

"Well, you don't say what you think of it," said one of the weavers.

"Oh, it's delightful—most exquisite!" said the old Chamberlain, looking through his spectacles. "What a wonderful design and what beautiful colors! I shall certainly tell the Emperor that I am enchanted with it."

"We're very pleased to hear that," said the two weavers, and they started describing the colors and the curious pattern. The old Chamberlain listened carefully in order to repeat, when he came home to the Emperor, exactly what he had heard, and he did so.

The swindlers now demanded more money, as well as more silk and gold thread, saying that they needed it for weaving. They put everything into their pockets and not a thread appeared upon the looms, but they kept on working at the empty frames as before.

Soon after this, the Emperor sent another nice official to see how the weaving was getting on and to inquire whether the stuff would soon be ready. Exactly the same thing happened to him as to the Chamberlain. He looked and looked, but as there was nothing to be seen except the empty looms, he could see nothing.

"Isn't it a beautiful piece of material?" said the swindlers, showing and describing the pattern that did not exist at all.

"Stupid I certainly am not," thought the official. "Then I must be unfit for my excellent post, I suppose. That seems rather funny—but I'll take great care that nobody gets wind of it." Then he praised the material he could not see and assured them of his enthusiasm for the gorgeous colors and the beautiful pattern. "It's simply enchanting!" he said to the Emperor.

The whole town was talking about the splendid material.

And now the Emperor was curious to see it for himself while it was still upon the looms.

Accompanied by a great number of selected people, among whom were the two nice old officials who had already been there, the Emperor went forth to visit the two wily swindlers. They were now weaving madly, yet without a single thread upon the looms.

"Isn't it magnificent?" said the two nice officials. "Will Your Imperial Majesty deign to look at this splendid pattern and these glorious colors?" Then they pointed to the empty looms, for each thought that the others could probably see the material.

"What on earth can this mean?" thought the Emperor. "I don't see anything! This is terrible. Am I stupid? Am I unfit to be Emperor? That would be the most disastrous thing that could possibly befall me.

"Oh, it's perfectly wonderful!" he said. "It quite meets with my Imperial approval." And he nodded appreciatively and stared at the empty looms—he would not admit that he saw nothing. His whole suite looked and looked, but with as little result as the others. Nevertheless, they all said, like the Emperor, "It's perfectly wonderful!" They advised him to have some new clothes made from this splendid stuff and to wear them for the first time in the next great procession.

"Magnificent!" "Excellent!" "Prodigious!" went from mouth to mouth, and everyone was exceedingly pleased. The Emperor gave each of the swindlers a decoration to wear in his buttonhole, and the title of "Knight of the Loom."

Before the procession they worked all night, burning more than sixteen candles. People could see how busy they were finishing the Emperor's new clothes. They pretended to take the material from the looms, they slashed the air with great scissors, they sewed with needles without any thread, and finally they said, "The Emperor's clothes are ready!"

Then the Emperor himself arrived with his most distinguished courtiers, and each swindler raised an arm as if he were holding something and said, "These are Your Imperial Majesty's knee-breeches. This is Your Imperial Majesty's robe. This is Your Imperial Majesty's mantle," and so forth. "It is all as light as a spider's web. One might fancy one had nothing on, but that is just the beauty of it!"

"Yes, indeed," said all the courtiers, but they could see nothing, for there was nothing to be seen.

"If Your Imperial Majesty would graciously consent to take off your clothes," said the swindlers, "we could fit on the new ones in front of the long glass."

13

So the Emperor laid aside his clothes, and the swindlers pretended to hand him, piece by piece, the new ones they were supposed to have made. And they fitted him round the waist and acted as if they were fastening something on—it was the train. And the Emperor turned round and round in front of the long glass.

"How well the new robes suit Your Imperial Majesty! How well they fit!" they all said. "What a splendid design! What gorgeous colors! It's all magnificently regal!"

"The canopy which is to be held over Your Imperial Majesty in the procession is waiting outside," announced the Lord High Chamberlain.

"Well, I suppose I'm ready," said the Emperor. "Don't you think they are a nice fit?" And he looked at himself again in the glass, first on one side and then the other, as if he really were carefully examining his handsome attire.

The courtiers who were to carry the train groped about on the floor with fumbling fingers and pretended to lift it. They walked on, holding their hands up in the air. Nothing would have induced them to admit that they could not see anything.

And so the Emperor set off in the procession under the beautiful canopy, and everybody in the streets and at the windows said, "Oh! how superb the Emperor's new cothes are! What a gorgeous train! What a perfect fit!" No one would acknowledge that he didn't see anything, so proving that he was not fit for his post, or that he was very stupid.

None of the Emperor's clothes had ever met with such a success.

"But he hasn't got any clothes on!" gasped out a little child.

"Good heavens! Hark at the little innocent!" said the father, and people whispered to one another what the child had said. "But he hasn't got any clothes on! There's a little child saying he hasn't got any clothes on!"

"But he hasn't got any clothes on!" shouted the whole town at last. The Emperor had a creepy feeling down his spine, because it began to dawn on him that the people were right. "All the same," he thought to himself, "I've got to go through with it as long as the procession lasts."

So he drew himself up and held his head higher than before, and the courtiers held on to the train that wasn't there at all.

The Devoted Friend

Oscar Wilde

One morning the old Water Rat put his head out of his hole. He had bright, beady eyes and stiff gray whiskers, and his tail was like a long bit of black india rubber. The little ducks were swimming about in the pond, looking just like a lot of yellow canaries, and their mother, who was pure white with real red legs, was trying to teach them how to stand on their heads in the water.

"You will never be in the best society unless you can stand on your heads," she kept saying to them, and every now and then she showed them how it was done. But the little ducks paid no attention to her. They were so young that they did not know what an advantage it is to be in society at all.

"What disobedient children!" cried the old Water Rat. "They really deserve to be drowned."

17

"Nothing of the kind," answered the Duck. "Everyone must make a beginning, and parents cannot be too patient."

"Ah! I know nothing about the feelings of parents," said the Water Rat. "I am not a family man. In fact, I have never been married, and I never intend to be. Love is all very well in its way, but friendship is much higher. Indeed, I know of nothing in the world that is either nobler or rarer than a devoted friendship."

"And what, pray, is your idea of the duties of a devoted friend?" asked a green Linnet, who was sitting on a willow tree hard by and had overheard the conversation.

"Yes, that is just what I want to know," said the Duck, and she swam away to the end of the pond and stood upon her head, in order to give her children a good example.

"What a silly question!" cried the Water Rat. "I should expect my devoted friend to be devoted to me, of course."

"And what would you do in return?" said the little bird, swinging upon a silver spray and flapping his tiny wings.

"I don't understand you," answered the Water Rat.

"Let me tell you a story on the subject," said the Linnet.

"Is the story about me?" asked the Water Rat. "If so, I will listen to it, for I am extremely fond of fiction."

"It is applicable to you," answered the Linnet. And he flew down, and, alighting upon the bank, he told the story of The Devoted Friend.

"Once upon a time," said the Linnet, "there was an honest little fellow named Hans."

"Was he very distinguished?" asked the Water Rat.

"No," answered the Linnet, "I don't think he was distinguished at all, except for his kind heart and his funny, round, good-humored face. He lived in a tiny cottage all by himself, and every day he worked in his garden. In all the countryside there was no garden so lovely as his. Sweet williams grew there, and gilly-flowers, and shepherd's purses, and fair-maids-of-France. There were damask roses, and yellow roses, lilac crocuses and gold, purple violets and white. columbine and lady's-smock, marjoram and wild basil, the cowslip and the flower-de-luce, the daffodil and the clove pink bloomed or blossomed in their proper order as the months went by, one flower taking another flower's place, so that there were always beautiful things to look at and pleasant odors to smell.

"Little Hans had a great many friends, but the most devoted friend of all was big Hugh the Miller. Indeed, so devoted was the rich Miller to little Hans, that he would never go by his garden without leaning over the wall and plucking a large nosegay, or a handful of sweet herbs, or filling his pockets with plums and cherries if it was the fruit season.

" 'Real friends should have everything in common,' the Miller used to say, and little Hans nodded and smiled, and felt very proud of having a friend with such noble ideas.

"Sometimes, indeed, the neighbors thought it strange that the rich Miller never gave little Hans anything in return, though he had a hundred sacks of flour stored away in his mill, and six milch cows, and a large flock of woolly sheep; but Hans never troubled his head about

19

these things, and nothing gave him greater pleasure than to listen to all the wonderful things the Miller used to say about the unselfishness of true friendship.

"So little Hans worked away in his garden. During the spring, the summer, and the autumn he was very happy, but when the winter came, and he had no fruit or flowers to bring to the market, he suffered a good deal from cold and hunger, and often had to go to bed without any supper but a few dried pears or some hard nuts. In the winter, also, he was extremely lonely, as the Miller never came to see him then.

" 'There is no good in my going to see little Hans as long as the snow lasts,' the Miller used to say to his wife, 'for when people are in trouble they should be left alone and not be bothered by visitors. That at least is my idea about friendship, and I am sure I am right. So I shall wait till the spring comes, and then I shall pay him a visit, and he will be able to give me a large basket of primroses, and that will make him so happy.'

" 'You are certainly very thoughtful about others,' answered the Wife, as she sat in her comfortable armchair by the big pinewood fire. 'Very thoughtful indeed. It is quite a treat to hear you talk about friendship. I am sure the clergyman himself could not say such beautiful things as you do, though he does live in a three-storied house and wear a gold ring on his little finger.'

" 'But could we not ask little Hans up here?' said the Miller's youngest son. 'If poor Hans is in trouble I will give him half my porridge and show him my white rabbits.'

" 'What a silly boy you are!' cried the Miller. 'I really

don't know what is the use of sending you to school. You seem not to learn anything. Why, if little Hans came up here and saw our warm fire and our good supper and our great cask of red wine, he might get envious, and envy is a most terrible thing, and would spoil anybody's nature. I certainly will not allow Hans' nature to be spoiled. I am his best friend, and I will always watch over him, and see that he is not led into any temptations. Besides, if Hans came here, he might ask me to let him have some flour on credit, and that I could not do. Flour is one thing, and friendship is another, and they should not be confused. Why, the words are spelled differently, and mean quite different things. Everybody can see that.'

" 'How well you talk!' said the Miller's Wife, pouring herself out a large glass of warm ale. 'Really I feel quite drowsy. It is just like being in church.'

" 'Lots of people act well,' answered the Miller, 'but very few people talk well, which shows that talking is much the more difficult thing of the two, and much the finer thing also.' And he looked sternly across the table at his little son, who felt so ashamed of himself that he hung his head down, and grew quite scarlet and began to cry into his tea. However, he was so young that you must excuse him."

"Is that the end of the story?" asked the Water Rat.

"Certainly not," answered the Linnet, "that is the beginning."

"Then you are quite behind the age," said the Water Rat. "Every good storyteller nowadays starts with the end, and then goes on to the beginning, and concludes with the middle. That is the new method. I heard all

21

about it the other day from a critic who was walking round the pond with a young man. He spoke of the matter at great length, and I am sure he must have been right, for he had blue spectacles and a bald head, and whenever the young man made any remark, he always answered 'Pooh!' But pray go on with your story. I like the Miller immensely. I have all kinds of beautiful sentiments myself, so there is a great sympathy between us."

"Well," said the Linnet, hopping now on one leg and now on the other, "as soon as the winter was over, and the primroses began to open their pale yellow stars, the Miller said to his Wife that he would go down and see little Hans.

" 'Why, what a good heart you have!' cried his Wife. 'You are always thinking of others. And mind you take the big basket with you for the flowers.'

"So the Miller tied the sails of the windmill together with a strong iron chain and went down the hill with the basket on his arm.

" 'Good morning, little Hans,' said the Miller.

" 'Good morning,' said Hans, leaning on his spade and smiling from ear to ear.

" 'And how have you been all the winter?' said the Miller.

" 'Well, really,' cried Hans, 'it is very good of you to ask, very good indeed. I am afraid I had rather a hard time of it, but now the spring has come, and I am quite happy, and all my flowers are doing well.'

" 'We often talked of you during the winter, Hans,' said the Miller, 'and wondered how you were getting on.'

" 'That was kind of you,' said Hans. 'I was half afraid you had forgotten me.'

" 'Hans, I am surprised at you,' said the Miller. 'Friendship never forgets. That is the wonderful thing about it. But I am afraid you won't understand the poetry of life. How lovely your primroses are looking, by-the-bye!'

" 'They are certainly very lovely,' said Hans, 'and it is a most lucky thing for me that I have so many. I am going to bring them into the market and sell them to the Burgomaster's daughter, and buy back my wheelbarrow with the money.'

" 'Buy back your wheelbarrow? You don't mean to say you have sold it? What a very stupid thing to do!'

" 'Well, the fact is,' said Hans, 'that I was obliged to. You see the winter was a very bad time for me, and I really had no money at all to buy bread with. So I first sold the silver buttons off my Sunday coat, and then I sold my silver chain, and then I sold my big pipe, and at last I sold my wheelbarrow. But I am going to buy them all back again now.'

" 'Hans,' said the Miller, 'I will give you my wheelbarrow. It is not in very good repair. Indeed, one side is gone, and there is something wrong with the wheelspokes, but in spite of that I will give it to you. I know it is very generous of me, and a great many people would think me extremely foolish for parting with it, but I am not like the rest of the world. I think that generosity is the essence of friendship, and, besides, I have got a new wheelbarrow for myself. Yes, you may set your mind at ease, I will give you my wheelbarrow.'

" 'Well, really, that is generous of you,' said little

Hans, and his funny round face glowed all over with pleasure. 'I can easily put it in repair, as I have a plank of wood in the house.'

" 'A plank of wood!' said the Miller. 'Why, that is just what I want for the roof of my barn. There is a very large hole in it, and the corn will all get damp if I don't stop it up. How lucky you mentioned it! It is quite remarkable how one good action always breeds another. I have given you my wheelbarrow, and now you are going to give me your plank. Of course, the wheelbarrow is worth far more than the plank, but true friendship never notices things like that. Pray get it at once, and I will set to work at my barn this very day.'

" 'Certainly,' cried little Hans, and he ran into the shed and dragged the plank out.

" 'It is not a very big plank,' said the Miller, looking at it, 'and I am afraid that after I have mended my barn roof there won't be any left for you to mend the wheelbarrow with; but, of course, that is not my fault. And now, as I have given you my wheelbarrow, I am sure you would like to give me some flowers in return. Here is the basket, and mind you fill it quite full.'

" 'Quite full?' said little Hans, rather sorrowfully, for it was really a very big basket, and he knew that if he filled it he would have no flowers left for the market, and he was very anxious to get his silver buttons back.

" 'Well, really,' answered the Miller, 'as I have given you my wheelbarrow, I don't think it is much to ask you for a few flowers. I may be wrong, but I should have thought that friendship, true friendship, was quite free from selfishness of any kind.'

" 'My dear friend, my best friend,' cried little Hans,

24

'you are welcome to all the flowers in my garden. I would much sooner have your good opinion than my silver buttons, any day.' And he ran and plucked all his pretty primroses and filled the Miller's basket.

" 'Good-bye, little Hans,' said the Miller, and he went up the hill with the plank on his shoulder and the big basket in his hand.

" 'Good-bye,' said little Hans, and he began to dig away quite merrily, he was so pleased about the wheelbarrow.

"The next day he was nailing up some honeysuckle against the porch, when he heard the Miller's voice calling to him from the road. So he jumped off the ladder, and ran down the garden, and looked over the wall.

"There was the Miller with a large sack of flour on his back.

" 'Dear little Hans,' said the Miller, 'would you mind carrying this sack of flour for me to market?'

" 'Oh, I am so sorry,' said Hans, 'but I am really very busy today. I have got all my creepers to nail up, and all my flowers to water, and all my grass to roll.'

" 'Well, really,' said the Miller, 'I think, that considering that I am going to give you my wheelbarrow, it is rather unfriendly of you to refuse.'

" 'Oh, don't say that,' cried little Hans. 'I wouldn't be unfriendly for the whole world.' And he ran in for his cap, and trudged off with the big sack on his shoulders.

"It was a very hot day, and the road was terribly dusty, and before Hans had reached the sixth milestone he was so tired that he had to sit down and rest. However, he went on bravely, and at last he reached the

25

market. After he had waited there for some time, he sold the sack of flour for a very good price, and then he returned home at once, for he was afraid that if he stopped too late he might meet some robbers on the way.

" 'It has certainly been a hard day,' said little Hans to himself as he was going to bed, 'but I am glad I did not refuse the Miller, for he is my best friend and, besides, he is going to give me his wheelbarrow.'

"Early the next morning the Miller came down to get the money for his sack of flour, but little Hans was so tired that he was still in bed.

" 'Upon my word,' said the Miller, 'you are very lazy. Really, considering that I am going to give you my wheelbarrow, I think you might work harder. Idleness is a great sin, and I certainly don't like any of my friends to be idle or sluggish. You must not mind my speaking quite plainly to you. Of course I should not dream of doing so if I were not your friend. But what is the good of friendship if one cannot say exactly what one means? Anybody can say charming things and try to please and to flatter, but a true friend always says unpleasant things and does not mind giving pain. Indeed, if he is a really true friend he prefers it, for he knows that then he is doing good.'

" 'I am very sorry,' said little Hans, rubbing his eyes and pulling off his nightcap, 'but I was so tired that I thought I would lie in bed for a little time and listen to the birds singing. Do you know that I always work better after hearing the birds sing?'

" 'Well, I am glad of that,' said the Miller, clapping little Hans on the back, 'for I want you to come up to

26

the mill as soon as you are dressed and mend my barn roof for me.'

"Poor little Hans was very anxious to go and work in his garden, for his flowers had not been watered for two days, but he did not like to refuse the Miller, as he was such a good friend to him.

" 'Do you think it would be unfriendly of me if I said I was busy?' he inquired in a shy and timid voice.

" 'Well, really,' answered the Miller, 'I do not think it is much to ask of you, considering that I am going to give you my wheelbarrow; but, of course, if you refuse I will go and do it myself.'

" 'Oh! on no account,' cried little Hans, and he jumped out of bed and dressed himself and went up to the barn.

"He worked there all day long, till sunset, and at sunset the Miller came to see how he was getting on.

" 'Have you mended the hole in the roof yet, little Hans?' cried the Miller in a cheery voice.

" 'It is quite mended,' answered little Hans, coming down the ladder.

" 'Ah!' said the Miller, 'there is no work so delightful as the work one does for others.'

" 'It is certainly a great privilege to hear you talk,' answered little Hans, sitting down and wiping his forehead, 'a very great privilege. But I am afraid I shall never have such beautiful ideas as you have.'

" 'Oh! they will come to you,' said the Miller, 'but you must take more pains. At present you have only the practice of friendship; some day you will have the theory also.'

" 'Do you really think I shall?' asked little Hans.

" 'I have no doubt of it,' answered the Miller, 'but now that you have mended the roof, you had better go home and rest, for I want you to drive my sheep to the mountain tomorrow.'

"Poor little Hans was afraid to say anything to this, and early the next morning the Miller brought his sheep round to the cottage, and Hans started off with them to the mountain. It took him the whole day to get there and back, and when he returned he was so tired that he went off to sleep in his chair and did not wake up till it was broad daylight.

" 'What a delightful time I shall have in my garden!' he said, and he went to work at once.

"But somehow he was never able to look after his flowers at all, for his friend the Miller was always coming round and sending him off on long errands, or getting him to help at the mill. Little Hans was very much distressed at times, as he was afraid his flowers would think he had forgotten them, but he consoled himself by the reflection that the Miller was his best friend. 'Besides,' he used to say, 'he is going to give me his wheelbarrow, and that is an act of pure generosity.'

"So little Hans worked away for the Miller, and the Miller said all kinds of beautiful things about friendship, which Hans took down in a notebook, and used to read over at night, for he was a very good scholar.

"Now it happened that one evening little Hans was sitting by his fireside when a loud rap came at the door. It was a very wild night, and the wind was blowing and roaring round the house so terribly that at first he thought it was merely the storm. But a second rap came, and then a third, louder than any of the others.

28

" 'It is some poor traveler,' said little Hans to himself, and he ran to the door.

"There stood the Miller with a lantern in one hand and a big stick in the other.

" 'Dear little Hans,' cried the Miller, 'I am in great trouble. My little boy has fallen off a ladder and hurt himself, and I am going for the Doctor. But he lives so far away, and it is such a bad night, that it has just occurred to me that it would be much better if you went instead of me. You know I am going to give you my wheelbarrow, and so it is only fair that you should do something for me in return.'

" 'Certainly,' cried little Hans, 'I take it quite as a compliment your coming to me, and I will start off at once. But you must lend me your lantern, as the night is so dark that I am afraid I might fall into the ditch.'

" 'I am very sorry,' answered the Miller, 'but it is my new lantern, and it would be a great loss to me if anything happened to it.'

" 'Well, never mind, I will do without it,' cried little Hans, and he took down his great fur coat, and his warm scarlet cap, and tied a muffler round his throat, and started off.

"What a dreadful storm it was! The night was so black that little Hans could hardly see, and the wind was so strong that he could hardly stand. However, he was very courageous, and after he had been walking about three hours, he arrived at the Doctor's house and knocked at the door.

" 'Who is there?' cried the Doctor, putting his head out of his bedroom window.

" 'Little Hans, Doctor.'

29

" 'What do you want, little Hans?'

" 'The Miller's son has fallen from a ladder and has hurt himself, and the Miller wants you to come at once.'

" 'All right!' said the Doctor. And he ordered his horse and his big boots and his lantern, and came downstairs, and rode off in the direction of the Miller's house, little Hans trudging behind him.

"But the storm grew worse and worse, and the rain fell in torrents, and little Hans could not see where he was going, or keep up with the horse. At last he lost his way and wandered off on the moor, which was a very dangerous place, as it was full of deep holes, and there poor little Hans was drowned. His body was found the next day by some goatherds, floating in a great pool of water, and was brought back by them to the cottage.

"Everybody went to little Hans' funeral, as he was so popular, and the Miller was the chief mourner.

" 'As I was his best friend,' said the Miller, 'it is only fair that I should have the best place.' So he walked at the head of the procession in a long black cloak, and every now and then he wiped his eyes with a big pocket-handkerchief.

" 'Little Hans is certainly a great loss to everyone,' said the Blacksmith when the funeral was over, and they were all seated comfortably in the inn, drinking spiced wine and eating sweet cakes.

" 'A great loss to me at any rate,' answered the Miller. 'Why, I had as good as given him my wheelbarrow, and now I really don't know what to do with it. It is very much in my way at home, and it is in such bad repair that I could not get anything for it if I sold it. I will certainly take care not to give away anything again. One certainly suffers for being generous.' "

"Well?" said the Water Rat, after a long pause.

"Well, that is the end," said the Linnet.

"But what became of the Miller?" asked the Water Rat.

"Oh! I really don't know," replied the Linnet. "And I am sure that I don't care."

"It is quite evident then that you have no sympathy in your nature," said the Water Rat.

"I am afraid that you don't quite see the moral of the story," remarked the Linnet.

"The what?" screamed the Water Rat.

"The moral."

"Do you mean to say that the story has a moral?"

"Certainly," said the Linnet.

"Well, really," said the Water Rat in a very angry manner, "I think you should have told me that before you began. If you had done so, I certainly would not have listened to you; in fact, I should have said 'Pooh,' like the critic. However, I can say it now." So he shouted out "Pooh" at the top of his voice, gave a whisk with his tail, and went back into his hole.

"And how do you like the Water Rat?" asked the Duck, who came paddling up some minutes afterwards. "He has a great many good points, but for my own part I have a mother's feelings, and I can never look at a confirmed bachelor without the tears coming into my eyes."

"I am rather afraid that I have annoyed him," answered the Linnet. "The fact is that I told him a story with a moral."

"Ah! that is always a very dangerous thing to do," said the Duck.

And I quite agree with her.

Allah Will Provide

An African Tale
Told by Robert Gilstrap
and Irene Estabrook

Bou Azza was an honest woodcutter who worked hard each day cutting down trees which he sold in the marketplace of a small North African village. His efforts were not highly rewarded, however, for he earned barely enough money to keep his young wife and himself in food and clothing.

Because he was getting old in body, Bou Azza wondered with each passing day how much longer he would be able to work and who would take care of him and his wife when he was too old to do so.

One afternoon as the hot sun beat down on him, Bou Azza gathered together the logs he had cut that morning, fastened them with a piece of rope, and slung them over his shoulder. Then he set out down the hill toward his tiny house on the outskirts of the village.

Before reaching his home, Bou was forced to stop and

rest beneath an olive tree near the road. As he wiped the perspiration from his forehead, he suddenly noticed a horned viper curled up on the ground a few feet away from him. At first the old woodcutter was very frightened, for he knew that a bite from this reptile would surely kill him. Carefully he climbed up to a high branch of the olive tree. But after watching the snake for a few seconds, Bou Azza realized that he had nothing to fear. The snake had other interests.

On one of the lower branches of the tree, not far from where Bou Azza was sitting, there was a small bird. The snake was staring at the bird with its beady black eyes, swaying its long, slender body back and forth, and occasionally spitting out its evil-looking, forked tongue.

At first the bird did not notice the snake, but when she did, her small feathery body was seized with helpless terror. Gripping the fragile little twig on which she rested, she tried to move her wings, but they were frozen with fear. She also tried to sound an alarm, but her beak opened and shut without a sound coming out.

As the snake swayed back and forth, Bou Azza realized that the bird had been hypnotized by the viper's movements, and he watched the two animals with weird fascination.

As Bou Azza looked down, the viper held the bird in its merciless stare, swaying from side to side like the pendulum of a clock, while the helpless victim became more and more paralyzed. Then suddenly the little bird fell from the branch and landed just a few inches from the snake. As Bou Azza watched, the snake ate its prey whole—feathers and all. Then, satisfied, it crawled away looking for new victims.

Bou Azza, rested from his journey but sickened by what he had just witnessed, headed for home with his wood on his back and an idea in his head.

As Bou Azza walked home in the twilight, he thought more and more about his idea. After a time he said to himself, "I am a fool! The serpent finds much food without really working for it, thanks to Allah, whereas I, a man, must work very hard in the hottest part of the day to earn just a mouthful of food. Allah alone is good, and with his help I will be like the serpent. No longer will I work so hard to get food when the serpent gets it for nothing. So shall it be."

And continuing on his way home, Bou Azza wore an expression of contentment over the new way of life that the serpent had revealed to him.

On the following morn, instead of rising before the sun made its way into the sky, Bou Azza stayed in bed until noon. Then he took his grass mat to the rear of the house, where he sat under a fig tree.

His wife became worried at his strange behavior, and when she saw that he obviously had no plans to work for the day, she went to him and said, "Bou Azza! What is wrong with you today? Are you not going to cut wood to sell in the market?"

"No, wife," said Bou Azza as he stretched in the sun. "I will not leave my mat even if I die of hunger. Yesterday I saw a serpent finding his food without working, and I have decided that if Allah feeds the serpents, he will provide me with my bread."

His anxious wife had no idea what her husband was talking about and thought he had gone mad.

"Please get up," she cried, and she tugged at his

clothing. But nothing she said or did made any difference, and when twilight came to Bou Azza's home, he was still resting on his mat.

The poor woman was sick with worry, for she had always counted on her husband for food and money. But when she realized that he would not change his mind, she hurried to the woods while there was still light to see and looked for mushrooms to sell at the market in the village.

She looked for hours, scraping away leaves, digging under fallen logs, searching everywhere. Suddenly, as she dug into some soft earth, her knife hit something hard buried beneath the surface of the ground. Rapidly she dug the dirt away and uncovered a metal cooking pot with a lid. After working for some time, she pried the lid off and discovered that the pot was filled with shimmering gold pieces.

The animals of the forest drew close to watch her struggle helplessly with the giant pot as she shouted with excitement. But it was too heavy for her to lift. She ran as fast as she could to the house, crying with happiness. "Oh, Bou Azza," she shouted. "I have found a whole pot of gold. Come with me. Help me bring it to the house."

Actually, Bou Azza was impressed with the thought of the gold. But he had made a promise to himself not to move, and now he could not lift his finger.

"Oh wife," he said, without opening his eyes. "If Allah saw fit to let you find such a treasure, surely he will give you the strength to carry it home. Personally, I have decided not to move an inch!"

This reply made his wife furious, and she ran to the

house of her brothers to see if they would help her carry the pot home. Naturally her brothers were delighted with the prospect of sharing so much gold, and they ran with Bou Azza's wife to the forest and helped her carry it home.

When she and her brothers reached her house with the giant pot spilling over with gold, she felt sure that her husband would get off his mat and help her count their fortune.

"Get up, you lazy lout!" she shouted as she stood over her husband, who slept peacefully on his straw bed. "I hope you have enough energy to come and count your riches."

"Did I not tell you?" he said sleepily. "I am not going to lift a finger until Allah drops fortunes on my head just as he showered gifts on the serpent."

"Just as you like," the angry wife said as she filled her skirt with hundreds of heavy gold pieces and poured them over her husband's head.

"Praise be to Allah!" her husband shouted as the gold pieces fell around him. "Praise be to the one and only Allah! Do you not now see, my wife, that serpents and men are all his creatures and he does provide for all of us?"

His wife did not understand, but she did know that for the rest of their lives she and her husband would live in luxury and that Bou Azza would never have to work again.

And every time someone came to visit them, Bou Azza told them this story, ending each time with the words, "Why work? Allah will provide."

And although his listeners felt that he was wrong, no one could contradict him.

Vasilissa the Beautiful

A Russian Tale
Told by Post Wheeler

In a certain Tsardom, across three times nine
kingdoms, beyond high mountain chains, there once
lived a merchant. He had been married for twelve years,
but in that time there had been born to him only one
child, a daughter, who from her cradle was called
Vasilissa the Beautiful. When the little girl was eight
years old the mother fell ill, and before many days it
was plain to be seen that she must die. So she called
her little daughter to her, and taking a tiny wooden doll
from under the blanket of the bed, put it into her hands
and said:

"My little Vasilissa, my dear daughter, listen to what
I say, remember well my last words and fail not to carry
out my wishes. I am dying, and with my blessing, I
leave to thee this little doll. It is very precious, for there
is no other like it in the whole world. Carry it always

39

about with thee in thy pocket and never show it to anyone. When evil threatens thee or sorrow befalls thee, go into a corner, take it from thy pocket and give it something to eat and drink. It will eat and drink a little, and then thou mayest tell it thy trouble and ask its advice, and it will tell thee how to act in thy time of need." So saying, she kissed her little daughter on the forehead, blessed her, and shortly after died.

Little Vasilissa grieved greatly for her mother, and her sorrow was so deep that when the dark night came, she lay in her bed and wept and did not sleep. At length she bethought herself of the tiny doll, so she rose and took it from the pocket of her gown and, finding a piece of wheat bread and a cup of kvass,* she set them before it and said: "There, my little doll, take it. Eat a little, and drink a little, and listen to my grief. My dear mother is dead and I am lonely for her."

Then the doll's eyes began to shine like fireflies, and suddenly it became alive. It ate a morsel of the bread and took a sip of the kvass, and when it had eaten and drunk, it said: "Don't weep, little Vasilissa. Grief is worst at night. Lie down, shut thine eyes, comfort thyself, and go to sleep. The morning is wiser than the evening." So Vasilissa the Beautiful lay down, comforted herself, and went to sleep, and the next day her grieving was not so deep and her tears were less bitter.

Now after the death of his wife, the merchant sorrowed for many days as was right, but at the end of that time he began to desire to marry again and to look

---

* *Kvass* is a mild beer drunk at meals by Russians of all ages.

about him for a suitable wife. This was not difficult to
find, for he had a fine house, with a stable of swift
horses, besides being a good man who gave much to the
poor. Of all the women he saw, however, the one who, to
his mind, suited him best of all was a widow of about
his own age with two daughters of her own, and she, he
thought, besides being a good housekeeper, would be a
kind foster mother to his little Vasilissa.

So the merchant married the widow and brought her
home as his wife, but the little girl soon found that her
foster mother was very far from being what her father
had thought. She was a cold, cruel woman who had
desired the merchant for the sake of his wealth and had
no love for his daughter. Vasilissa was the greatest
beauty in the whole village, while her own daughters
were as spare and homely as two crows, and because of
this all three envied and hated her. They gave her all
sorts of errands to run and difficult tasks to perform, in
order that the toil might make her thin and worn and
that her face might grow brown from sun and wind, and
they treated her so cruelly as to leave few joys in life for
her. But all this the little Vasilissa endured without
complaint, and while the stepmother's two daughters
grew always thinner and uglier, in spite of the fact that
they had no hard tasks to do, never went out in cold or
rain, and sat always with their arms folded like ladies of
a Court, she herself had cheeks like blood and milk and
grew every day more and more beautiful.

Now the reason for this was the tiny doll, without
whose help little Vasilissa could never have managed to
do all the work that was laid upon her. Each night,
when everyone else was sound asleep, she would get up

41

from her bed, take the doll into a closet, and locking the door, give it something to eat and drink, and say: "There, my little doll, take it. Eat a little, drink a little, and listen to my grief. I live in my father's house, but my spiteful stepmother wishes to drive me out of the white world. Tell me! How shall I act, and what shall I do?"

Then the little doll's eyes would begin to shine like glowworms, and it would become alive. It would eat a little food, and sip a little drink, and then it would comfort her and tell her how to act. While Vasilissa slept, it would get ready all her work for the next day, so that she had only to rest in the shade and gather flowers, for the doll would have the kitchen garden weeded, and the beds of cabbage watered, and plenty of fresh water brought from the well, and the stoves heated exactly right. And, besides this, the little doll told her how to make, from a certain herb, an ointment which prevented her from ever being sunburned. So all the joy in life that came to Vasilissa came to her through the tiny doll that she always carried in her pocket.

Years passed, till Vasilissa grew up and became of an age when it is good to marry. All the young men in the village, high and low, rich and poor, asked for her hand, while not one of them stopped even to look at the stepmother's two daughters, so ill-favored were they. This angered their mother still more against Vasilissa. She answered every gallant who came with the same words: "Never shall the younger be wed before the older ones!" And each time, when she had let a suitor out of the door, she would soothe her anger and hatred by

42

beating her stepdaughter. So while Vasilissa grew each day more lovely and graceful, she was often miserable, and but for the little doll in her pocket, would have longed to leave the white world.

Now there came a time when it became necessary for the merchant to leave his home and to travel to a distant Tsardom. He bade farewell to his wife and her two daughters, kissed Vasilissa and gave her his blessing, and departed, bidding them say a prayer each day for his safe return. Scarce was he out of sight of the village, however, when his wife sold his house, packed all his goods, and moved with them to another dwelling far from the town, in a gloomy neighborhood on the edge of a wild forest. Here every day, while her two daughters were working indoors, the merchant's wife would send Vasilissa on one errand or other into the forest, either to find a branch of a certain rare bush or to bring her flowers or berries.

Now deep in this forest, as the stepmother well knew, there was a green lawn, and on the lawn stood a miserable little hut on hens' legs, where lived a certain Baba-Yaga, an old witch grandmother. She lived alone and none dared go near the hut, for she ate people as one eats chickens. The merchant's wife sent Vasilissa into the forest each day, hoping she might meet the old witch and be devoured. But always the girl came home safe and sound, because the little doll showed her where the bush, the flowers, and the berries grew, and did not let her go near the hut that stood on hens' legs. And each time the stepmother hated her more and more because she came to no harm.

One autumn evening the merchant's wife called the

43

three girls to her and gave them each a task. One of her daughters she bade make a piece of lace, the other to knit a pair of hose, and to Vasilissa she gave a basket of flax to be spun. She bade each finish a certain amount. Then she put out all the fires in the house, leaving only a single candle lighted in the room where the three girls worked, and she herself went to sleep.

They worked an hour, they worked two hours, they worked three hours, when one of the elder daughters took up the tongs to straighten the wick of the candle. She pretended to do this awkwardly (as her mother had bidden her) and put the candle out, as if by accident.

"What are we to do now?" asked her sister. "The fires are all out, there is no other light in all the house, and our tasks are not done."

"We must go and fetch fire," said the first. "The only house near is a hut in the forest, where a Baba-Yaga lives. One of us must go and borrow fire from her."

"I have enough light from my steel pins," said the one who was making the lace, "and *I* will not go."

"And I have plenty of light from my silver needles," said the other, who was knitting the hose, "and *I* will not go."

"Thou, Vasilissa," they both said, "shalt go and fetch the fire, for thou hast neither steel pins nor silver needles and cannot see to spin thy flax!" They both rose up, pushed Vasilissa out of the house and locked the door, crying: "Thou shalt not come in till thou hast fetched the fire."

Vasilissa sat down on the doorstep, took the tiny doll from one pocket and from another the supper she had ready for it, put the food before it, and said: "There, my

little doll, take it. Eat a little and listen to my sorrow. I
must go to the hut of the old Baba-Yaga in the dark
forest to borrow some fire, and I fear she will eat me.
Tell me! What shall I do?"

Then the doll's eyes began to shine like two stars and
it became alive. It ate a little and said: "Do not fear,
little Vasilissa. Go where thou hast been sent. While I
am with thee no harm shall come to thee from the old
witch." So Vasilissa put the doll back into her pocket,
crossed herself, and started out into the dark, wild
forest.

Whether she walked a short way or a long way the
telling is easy, but the journey was hard. The wood was
very dark, and she could not help trembling from fear.
Suddenly she heard the sound of a horse's hoofs, and a
man on horseback galloped past her. He was dressed all
in white, the horse under him was milk-white and the
harness was white, and just as he passed her it became
twilight.

She went a little farther, and again she heard the
sound of horse's hoofs, and there came another man on
horseback galloping past her. He was dressed all in red,
and the horse under him was blood-red and its harness
was red, and just as he passed her the sun rose.

That whole day Vasilissa walked, for she had lost her
way. She could find no path at all in the dark wood, and
she had no food to set before the little doll to make it
alive.

But at evening she came all at once to the green lawn
where the wretched little hut stood on its hens' legs.
The wall around the hut was made of human bones, and
on its top were skulls. There was a gate in the wall,

45

whose hinges were the bones of human feet and whose locks were jawbones set with sharp teeth. The sight filled Vasilissa with horror, and she stopped as still as a post buried in the ground.

As she stood there, a third man on horseback came galloping up. His face was black, he was dressed all in black, and the horse he rode was coal-black. He galloped up to the gate of the hut and disappeared there as if he had sunk through the ground, and at that moment the night came and the forest grew dark.

But it was not dark on the green lawn, for instantly the eyes of all the skulls on the wall were lighted up and shone till the place was as bright as day. When she saw this Vasilissa trembled so with fear that she could not run away.

Then suddenly the wood became full of a terrible noise. The trees began to groan, the branches to creak and the dry leaves to rustle, and the Baba-Yaga came flying from the forest. She was riding in a great iron mortar and driving it with the pestle,* and as she came she swept away her trail behind her with a kitchen broom.

She rode up to the gate, and stopping, said:

> Little House, little House,
> Stand the way thy mother placed thee,
> Turn thy back to the forest and thy face to me!

And the little hut turned facing her and stood still. Then smelling all around her, she cried: "Foo! Foo! I smell a smell that is Russian. Who is here?"

---

* *Mortar and pestle.* A mortar is a deep, sturdy bowl in which grains, herbs, and spices are crushed. The small, club-shaped grinding tool is called a pestle.

46

Vasilissa, in great fright, came nearer to the old woman and, bowing very low, said: "It is only Vasilissa, grandmother. My stepmother's daughters sent me to thee to borrow some fire."

"Well," said the old witch, "I know them. But if I give thee the fire thou shalt stay with me some time and do some work to pay for it. If not, thou shalt be eaten for my supper." Then she turned to the gate and shouted: "Ho! Ye, my solid locks, unlock! Thou, my stout gate, open!" Instantly the locks unlocked, the gate opened of itself, and the Baba-Yaga rode in whistling. Vasilissa entered behind her, and immediately the gate shut again and the locks snapped tight.

When they had entered the hut the old witch threw herself down on the stove, stretched out her bony legs, and said: "Come, fetch and put on the table at once everything that is in the oven. I am hungry." So Vasilissa ran and lighted a splinter of wood from one of the skulls on the wall, and took the food from the oven and set it before her. There was enough cooked meat for three strong men. She brought also from the cellar kvass, honey, and red wine, and the Baba-Yaga ate and drank the whole, leaving the girl only a little cabbage soup, a crust of bread, and a morsel of suckling pig.

When her hunger was satisfied, the old witch, growing drowsy, lay down on the stove and said: "Listen to me well, and do what I bid thee. Tomorrow when I drive away, do thou clean the yard, sweep the floors, and cook my supper. Then take a quarter of a measure of wheat from my storehouse and pick out of it all the black grains and the wild peas. Mind thou dost all that I have bade. If not, thou shalt be eaten for my supper."

47

Presently the Baba-Yaga turned toward the wall and began to snore, and Vasilissa knew that she was fast asleep. Then she went into the corner, took the tiny doll from her pocket, put before it a bit of bread and a little cabbage soup that she had saved, burst into tears and said: "There, my little doll, take it. Eat a little, drink a little, and listen to my grief. Here I am in the house of the old witch, and the gate in the wall is locked, and I am afraid. She has given me a difficult task, and if I do not do all she has bade, she will eat me tomorrow. Tell me: What shall I do?"

Then the eyes of the little doll began to shine like two candles. It ate a little of the bread and drank a little of the soup and said: "Do not be afraid, Vasilissa the Beautiful. Be comforted. Say thy prayers, and go to sleep. The morning is wiser than the evening." So Vasilissa trusted the little doll and was comforted. She said her prayers, lay down on the floor, and went fast asleep.

When she woke next morning, very early, it was still dark. She rose and looked out of the window, and she saw that the eyes of the skulls on the wall were growing dim. As she looked, the man dressed all in white, riding the milk-white horse, galloped swiftly around the corner of the hut, leaped the wall and disappeared, and as he went, it became quite light and the eyes of the skulls flickered and went out. The old witch was in the yard. Now she began to whistle and the great iron mortar and pestle and the kitchen broom flew out of the hut to her. As she got into the mortar the man dressed all in red, mounted on the blood-red horse, galloped like the wind around the corner of the hut, leaped the wall and was gone, and at that moment the sun rose. Then the Baba-Yaga shouted: "Ho! Ye, my solid locks, unlock! Thou, my stout gate, open!" And the locks unlocked and the gate opened, and she rode away in the mortar, driving with the pestle and sweeping away her path behind her with the broom.

When Vasilissa found herself left alone, she examined the hut, wondering to find it filled with such an abundance of everything. Then she stood still, remembering all the work that she had been bidden to do and wondering what to begin first. But as she looked she rubbed her eyes, for the yard was already neatly cleaned and the floors were nicely swept, and the little doll was sitting in the storehouse picking the last black grains and wild peas out of the quarter-measure of wheat.

Vasilissa ran and took the little doll in her arms. "My dearest little doll!" she cried. "Thou has saved me from my trouble! Now I have only to cook the Baba-Yaga's supper, since all the rest of the tasks are done!"

"Cook it, with God's help," said the doll, "and then rest, and may the cooking of it make thee healthy!" And so saying it crept into her pocket and became again only a little wooden doll.

So Vasilissa rested all day and was refreshed, and when it grew toward evening she laid the table for the old witch's supper and sat looking out of the window, waiting for her coming. After a while she heard the sound of a horse's hoofs, and the man in black, on a coal-black horse, galloped up to the wall gate and disappeared like a great dark shadow, and instantly it became quite dark and the eyes of all the skulls began to glitter and shine.

Then all at once the trees of the forest began to creak and groan, and the leaves and the bushes to moan and sigh, and the Baba-Yaga came riding out of the dark wood in the huge iron mortar, driving with the pestle and sweeping out the trail behind her with the kitchen broom. Vasilissa let her in, and the witch, smelling all around her, asked: "Well, hast thou done perfectly all the tasks I gave thee to do, or am I to eat thee for my supper?"

"Be so good as to look for thyself, grandmother," answered Vasilissa.

The Baba-Yaga went all about the place tapping with her iron pestle and carefully examining everything. But so well had the little doll done its work that, try as hard as she might, she could not find anything to complain of. There was not a weed left in the yard, nor a speck of dust on the floors, nor a single black grain or wild pea in the wheat.

The old witch was greatly angered, but was obliged to pretend to be pleased. "Well," she said, "thou hast done all well." Then, clapping her hands, she shouted: "Ho! my faithful servants! Friends of my heart! Haste and grind my wheat!" Immediately three pairs of hands appeared, seized the measure of wheat, and carried it away.

The Baba-Yaga sat down to supper, and Vasilissa put before her all the food from the oven, with kvass, honey, and red wine. The old witch ate it, bones and all, almost to the last morsel, enough for four strong men. And then, growing drowsy, she stretched her bony legs on the stove and said: "Tomorrow do as thou hast done today, and besides these tasks take from my storehouse

50

a half-measure of poppy seeds and clean them one by one. Someone has mixed earth with them to do me a mischief and to anger me, and I will have them made perfectly clean." So saying she turned to the wall and soon began to snore.

When she was fast asleep Vasilissa went into the corner, took the little doll from her pocket, set before it a part of the food that was left, and asked its advice. And the doll, when it had become alive and eaten a little food and sipped a little drink, said: "Don't worry, beautiful Vasilissa! Be comforted. Do as thou didst last night: say thy prayers and go to sleep." So Vasilissa was comforted. She said her prayers and went to sleep and did not wake till next morning, when she heard the old witch in the yard whistling. She ran to the window just in time to see her take her place in the big iron mortar, and as she did so the man dressed all in red, riding on the blood-red horse, leaped over the wall and was gone, just as the sun rose over the wild forest.

As it had happened on the first morning, so it happened now. When Vasilissa looked she found that the little doll had finished all the tasks except the cooking of the supper. The yard was swept and in order, the floors were as clean as new wood, and there was not a grain of earth left in the half-measure of poppy seeds. She rested and refreshed herself till the afternoon, when she cooked the supper, and when evening came she laid the table and sat down to wait for the old witch's coming.

Soon the man in black, on the coal-black horse, galloped up to the gate, and the dark fell and the eyes of the skulls began to shine like day. Then the ground began to quake, and the trees of the forest began to creak and the dry leaves to rustle, and the Baba-Yaga came riding in her iron mortar, driving with her pestle and sweeping away her path with her broom.

When she came in she smelled around her and went all about the hut, tapping with the pestle. But pry and examine as she might, again she could see no reason to find fault and was angrier than ever. She clapped her hands and shouted: "Ho! my trusty servants! Friends of my soul! Haste and press the oil out of my poppy seeds!" And instantly the three pairs of hands appeared, seized the measure of poppy seeds, and carried it away.

Presently the old witch sat down to supper and Vasilissa brought all she had cooked, enough for five grown men, and set it before her, and brought beer and honey, and then she herself stood silently waiting. The Baba-Yaga ate and drank it all, every morsel, leaving not so much as a crumb of bread. Then she said snappishly: "Well, why dost thou say nothing, but stand there as if thou was dumb?"

"I spoke not," Vasilissa answered, "because I dared not. But if thou wilt allow me, grandmother, I wish to ask thee some questions."

"Well," said the old witch, "only remember that every question does not lead to good. If thou knowest overmuch, thou wilt grow old too soon. What wilt thou ask?"

"I would ask thee," said Vasilissa, "of the men on horseback. When I came to thy hut, a rider passed me. He was dressed all in white and he rode a milk-white horse. Who was he?"

"That was my white, bright day," answered the Baba-

52

Yaga angrily. "He is a servant of mine, but he cannot hurt thee. Ask me more."

"Afterwards," said Vasilissa, "a second rider overtook me. He was dressed in red and the horse he rode was blood-red. Who was he?"

"That was my servant, the round, red sun," answered the Baba-Yaga, "and he, too, cannot injure thee." And she ground her teeth. "Ask me more."

"A third rider," said Vasilissa, "came galloping up to the gate. He was black, his clothes were black, and the horse was coal-black. Who was he?"

"That was my servant, the black, dark night," answered the old witch furiously. "But he also cannot harm thee. Ask me more."

But Vasilissa, remembering what the Baba-Yaga had said, that not every question led to good, was silent.

"Ask me more!" cried the old witch. "Why dost thou not ask me more? Ask me of the three pairs of hands that serve me!"

But Vasilissa saw how she snarled at her and she answered: "The three questions are enough for me. As thou hast said, grandmother, I would not, through knowing overmuch, become too soon old."

"It is well for thee," said the Baba-Yaga, "that thou didst not ask of them, but only of what thou didst see outside of this hut. Hadst thou asked of them, my servants the three pairs of hands would have seized thee also, as they did the wheat and poppy seeds, to be my food. Now I would ask a question in my turn: How is it that thou hast been able, in a little time, to do perfectly all the tasks I gave thee? Tell me!"

Vasilissa was so frightened to see how the old witch

ground her teeth that she almost told her of the little doll. But she bethought herself just in time, and answered: "The blessing of my dead mother helps me."

Then the Baba-Yaga sprang up in a fury. "Get thee out of my house this moment!" she shrieked. "I want no one who bears a blessing to cross my threshold! Get thee gone!"

Vasilissa ran to the yard, and behind her she heard the old witch shouting to the locks and the gate. The locks opened, the gate swung wide, and she ran out on to the lawn. The Baba-Yaga seized from the wall one of the skulls with burning eyes and flung it after her. "There," she howled, "is the fire for thy stepmother's daughters. Take it. That is what they sent thee here for, and may they have joy of it!"

Vasilissa put the skull on the end of a stick and darted away through the forest, running as fast as she could and finding her path by the skull's glowing eyes, which went out only when morning came.

Whether she ran a long way or a short way, and whether the road was smooth or rough, towards evening of the next day, when the eyes in the skull were beginning to glimmer, she came out of the dark, wild forest to her stepmother's house.

When she came near the gate, she thought, "Surely, by this time they will have found some fire," and threw the skull into the hedge. But it spoke to her, and said: "Do not throw me away, beautiful Vasilissa. Bring me to thy stepmother." So, looking at the house and seeing no spark of light in any of the windows, she took up the skull again and carried it with her.

Now since Vasilissa had gone, the stepmother and her

54

two daughters had had neither fire nor light in all the house. When they struck flint and steel the tinder would not catch, and the fire they brought from the neighbors would go out immediately as soon as they carried it over the threshold, so that they had been unable to light or warm themselves or to cook food to eat. Therefore now, for the first time in her life, Vasilissa found herself welcomed. They opened the door to her, and the merchant's wife was greatly rejoiced to find that the light in the skull did not go out as soon as it was brought in. "Maybe the witch's fire will stay," she said, and took the skull into the best room, set it on a candlestick, and called her two daughters to admire it.

But the eyes of the skull suddenly began to glimmer and to glow like red coals, and wherever the three turned or ran the eyes followed them, growing larger and brighter till they flamed like two furnaces, and hotter and hotter till the merchant's wife and her two wicked daughters took fire and were burned to ashes. Only Vasilissa the Beautiful was not touched.

In the morning Vasilissa dug a deep hole in the ground and buried the skull. Then she locked the house and set out to the village, where she went to live with an old woman who was poor and childless. And so she remained for many days, waiting for her father's return from the far-distant Tsardom.

But, sitting lonely, time soon began to hang heavy on her hands. One day she said to the old woman: "It is dull for me, grandmother, to sit idly hour by hour. My hands want work to do. Go, therefore, and buy me some flax, the best and finest to be found anywhere, and at least I can spin."

The old woman hastened and bought some flax of the best sort, and Vasilissa sat down to work. So well did she spin that the thread came out as even and fine as a hair, and presently there was enough to begin to weave. But so fine was the thread that no frame could be found to weave it upon, nor would any weaver undertake to make one.

Then Vasilissa went into her closet, took the little doll from her pocket, set food and drink before it, and asked its help. And after it had eaten a little and drunk a little, the doll became alive and said: "Bring me an old frame and an old basket and some hairs from a horse's mane, and I will arrange everything for thee." Vasilissa hastened to fetch all the doll had asked for, and when evening came she said her prayers and went to sleep. In the morning she found ready a frame, perfectly made, to weave her fine thread upon.

She wove one month, she wove two months—all the winter Vasilissa sat weaving, weaving her fine thread, till the whole piece of linen was done, of a texture so fine that it could be passed, like thread, through the eye of a needle. When the spring came she bleached it so white that no snow could be compared with it. Then she said to the old woman: "Take thou the linen to the market, grandmother, and sell it, and the money shall suffice to pay for my food and lodging." When the old woman examined the linen, however, she said: "Never will I sell such cloth in the marketplace. No one should wear it except it be the Tsar himself, and tomorrow I shall carry it to the Palace."

Next day, accordingly, the old woman went to the Tsar's splendid Palace and fell to walking up and down before the windows. The servants came to ask her her errand, but she answered them nothing and kept walking up and down. At length the Tsar opened his window and asked: "What dost thou want, old woman, that thou walkest here?"

"O Tsar's Majesty!" the old woman answered, "I have with me a marvelous piece of linen stuff, so wondrously woven that I will show it to none but thee."

The Tsar bade them bring her before him, and when he saw the linen he was struck with astonishment at its fineness and beauty. "What wilt thou take for it, old woman?" he asked.

"There is no price that can buy it, Little Father Tsar," she answered, "but I have brought it to thee as a gift." The Tsar could not thank the old woman enough. He took the linen and sent her to her house with many rich presents.

Seamstresses were called to make shirts for him out of the cloth, but when it had been cut up it was so fine that no one of them was deft and skillful enough to sew it. The best seamstresses in all the Tsardom were summoned but none dared undertake it. So at last the Tsar sent for the old woman and said: "If thou didst know how to spin such thread and weave such linen, thou must also know how to sew me shirts from it."

And the old woman answered: "O Tsar's Majesty, it was not I who wove the linen. It is the work of my adopted daughter."

"Take it, then," the Tsar said, "and bid her do it for me."

The old woman brought the linen home and told Vasilissa the Tsar's command. "Well I knew that the

57

work would needs be done by my own hands," said Vasilissa and, locking herself in her own room, began to make the shirts. So fast and well did she work that soon a dozen were ready. Then the old woman carried them to the Tsar, while Vasilissa washed her face, dressed her hair, put on her best gown, and sat down at the window to see what would happen. And presently a servant in the livery of the Palace came to the house and entering, said: "The Tsar, our lord, desires himself to see the clever needlewoman who has made his shirts and to reward her with his own hands."

Vasilissa rose and went at once to the Palace, and as soon as the Tsar saw her, he fell in love with her with all his soul. He took her by her white hand and made her sit beside him. "Beautiful maiden," he said, "never will I part from thee and thou shalt be my wife."

So the Tsar and Vasilissa the Beautiful were married, and her father returned from the far-distant Tsardom, and he and the old woman lived always with her in the splendid Palace, in all joy and contentment. And as for the little wooden doll, she carried it about with her in her pocket all her life long.

The Story of Dr. Dolittle

Hugh Lofting

The First Chapter

Puddleby

Once upon a time, many years ago—when our grandfathers were little children—there was a doctor; and his name was Dolittle—John Dolittle, M.D. "M.D." means that he was a proper doctor and knew a whole lot.

He lived in a little town called Puddleby-on-the-Marsh. All the folks, young and old, knew him well by sight. And whenever he walked down the street in his high hat everyone would say, "There goes the Doctor!— He's a clever man." And the dogs and the children would all run up and follow behind him; and even the crows that lived in the church tower would caw and nod their heads.

The house he lived in, on the edge of the town, was quite small; but his garden was very large and had a wide lawn and stone seats and weeping willows hanging over. His sister, Sarah Dolittle, was housekeeper for him; but the Doctor looked after the garden himself.

He was very fond of animals and kept many kinds of pets. Besides the goldfish in the pond at the bottom of his garden, he had rabbits in the pantry, white mice in his piano, a squirrel in the linen closet, and a hedgehog in the cellar. He had a cow with a calf too, and an old lame horse—twenty-five years of age—and chickens, and pigeons, and two lambs, and many other animals. But his favorite pets were Dab-Dab the duck, Jip the dog, Gub-Gub the baby pig, Polynesia the parrot, and the owl Too-Too.

His sister used to grumble about all these animals and said they made the house untidy. And one day when an old lady with rheumatism came to see the Doctor, she sat on the hedgehog who was sleeping on the sofa and never came to see him any more, but drove every Saturday all the way to Oxenthorpe, another town ten miles off, to see a different doctor.

Then his sister, Sarah Dolittle, came to him and said:

"John, how can you expect sick people to come and see you when you keep all these animals in the house? It's a fine doctor would have his parlor full of hedgehogs and mice! That's the fourth personage these animals have driven away. Squire Jenkins and the Parson say they wouldn't come near your house again—no matter how sick they are. We are getting poorer every day. If you go on like this, none of the best people will have you for a doctor."

"But I like the animals better than the 'best people,'" said the Doctor.

"You are ridiculous," said his sister, and walked out of the room.

So, as time went on, the Doctor got more and more animals; and the people who came to see him got less and less. Till at last he had no one left—except the Cat's-meat-Man, who didn't mind any kind of animals. But the Cat's-meat-Man wasn't very rich and he only got sick once a year—at Christmastime, when he used to give the Doctor sixpence for a bottle of medicine.

Sixpence a year wasn't enough to live on—even in those days, long ago; and if the Doctor hadn't had some money saved up in his money-box, no one knows what would have happened.

And he kept on getting still more pets; and of course it cost a lot to feed them. And the money he had saved up grew littler and littler.

Then he sold his piano and let the mice live in a bureau drawer. But the money he got for that too began to go, so he sold the brown suit he wore on Sundays and went on becoming poorer and poorer.

And now, when he walked down the street in his high hat, people would say to one another, "There goes John Dolittle, M.D.! There was a time when he was the best-known doctor in the West Country. Look at him now—he hasn't any money and his stockings are full of holes!"

But the dogs and the cats and the children still ran up and followed him through the town—the same as they had done when he was rich.

The Second Chapter
Animal Language

It happened one day that the Doctor was sitting in his kitchen talking with the Cat's-meat-Man who had come to see him with a stomachache.

"Why don't you give up being a people's doctor and be an animal doctor?" asked the Cat's-meat-Man.

The parrot, Polynesia, was sitting in the window looking out at the rain and singing a sailor song to herself. She stopped singing and started to listen.

"You see, Doctor," the Cat's-meat-Man went on, "you know all about animals—much more than what these here vets do. That book you wrote—about cats, why, it's wonderful! I can't read or write myself—or maybe *I'd* write some books. But my wife, Theodosia, she's a scholar, she is. And she read your book to me. Well, it's wonderful—that's all can be said—wonderful. You might have been a cat yourself. You know the way they think. And listen: you can make a lot of money doctoring animals. Do you know that? You see, I'd send all the old women who had sick cats or dogs to you. And if they didn't get sick fast enough, I could put something in the meat I sell 'em to make 'em sick, see?"

"Oh, no," said the Doctor quickly. "You mustn't do that. That wouldn't be right."

"Oh, I didn't mean real sick," answered the Cat's-meat-Man. "Just a little something to make them droopy-like was what I had reference to. But as you say, maybe it ain't quite fair on the animals. But they'll get sick anyway, because the old women always give 'em too much to eat. And look, all the farmers 'round about who had lame horses and weak lambs—they'd come. Be an animal doctor."

When the Cat's-meat-Man had gone the parrot flew off the window onto the Doctor's table and said,

"That man's got sense. That's what you ought to do. Be an animal doctor. Give the silly people up—if they haven't brains enough to see you're the best doctor in the world. Take care of animals instead—*they'll* soon find it out. Be an animal doctor."

"Oh, there are plenty of animal doctors," said John Dolittle, putting the flowerpots outside on the windowsill to get the rain.

"Yes, there *are* plenty," said Polynesia. "But none of them are any good at all. Now listen, Doctor, and I'll tell you something. Did you know that animals can talk?"

"I knew that parrots can talk," said the Doctor.

"Oh, we parrots can talk in two languages—people's language and bird language," said Polynesia proudly. "If I say, 'Polly wants a cracker,' you understand me. But hear this: *Ka-ka oi-ee, fee-fee?*"

"Good Gracious!" cried the Doctor. "What does that mean?"

"That means, 'Is the porridge hot yet?'—in bird language."

"My! You don't say so!" said the Doctor. "You never talked that way to me before."

"What would have been the good?" said Polynesia, dusting some cracker crumbs off her left wing. "You wouldn't have understood me if I had."

"Tell me some more," said the Doctor, all excited; and he rushed over to the dresser drawer and came back with the butcher's book and a pencil. "Now don't go too fast—and I'll write it down. This is interesting—very interesting—something quite new. Give me the Birds' A.B.C. first—slowly now."

So that was the way the Doctor came to know that animals had a language of their own and could talk to one another. And all that afternoon, while it was raining, Polynesia sat on the kitchen table giving him bird words to put down in the book.

At teatime, when the dog, Jip, came in, the parrot said to the Doctor, "See, *he's* talking to you."

"Looks to me as though he were scratching his ear," said the Doctor.

"But animals don't always speak with their mouths," said the parrot in a high voice, raising her eyebrows. "They talk with their ears, with their feet, with their tails—with everything. Sometimes they don't *want* to make a noise. Do you see now the way he's twitching up one side of his nose?"

"What's that mean?" asked the Doctor.

"That means, 'Can't you see that it has stopped raining?' " Polynesia answered. "He is asking you a question. Dogs nearly always use their noses for asking questions."

After a while, with the parrot's help, the Doctor got to learn the language of the animals so well that he could talk to them himself and understand everything they said. Then he gave up being a people's doctor altogether.

As soon as the Cat's-meat-Man had told everyone that John Dolittle was going to become an animal doctor, old ladies began to bring him their pet pugs and poodles who had eaten too much cake; and farmers came many miles to show him sick cows and sheep.

One day a plow horse was brought to him; and the poor thing was terribly glad to find a man who could talk in horse language.

"You know, Doctor," said the horse, "that vet over

the hill knows nothing at all. He has been treating me six weeks now—for spavins.* What I need is *spectacles*. I am going blind in one eye. There's no reason why horses shouldn't wear glasses, the same as people. But that stupid man over the hill never even looked at my eyes. He kept on giving me big pills. I tried to tell him; but he couldn't understand a word of horse language. What I need is spectacles."

"Of course—of course," said the Doctor. "I'll get you some at once."

"I would like a pair like yours," said the horse—"only green. They'll keep the sun out of my eyes while I'm plowing the Fifty-Acre Field."

"Certainly," said the Doctor. "Green ones you shall have."

"You know, the trouble is, Sir," said the plow horse as the Doctor opened the front door to let him out—"the trouble is that *anybody* thinks he can doctor animals—just because the animals don't complain. As a matter of fact it takes a much cleverer man to be a really good animal doctor than it does to be a good people's doctor. My farmer's boy thinks he knows all about horses. I wish you could see him—his face is so fat he looks as though he had no eyes—and he has got as much brain as a potato bug. He tried to put a mustard plaster on me last week."

"Where did he put it?" asked the Doctor.

"Oh, he didn't put it anywhere—on me," said the horse. "He only tried to. I kicked him into the duck pond."

---

* *spavins*. A disease that makes horses lame.

"Well, well!" said the Doctor.

"I'm a pretty quiet creature as a rule," said the horse—"very patient with people—don't make much fuss. But it was bad enough to have that vet giving me the wrong medicine. And when that red-faced booby started to monkey with me, I just couldn't bear it any more."

"Did you hurt the boy much?" asked the Doctor.

"Oh, no," said the horse. "I kicked him in the right place. The vet's looking after him now. When will my glasses be ready?"

"I'll have them for you next week," said the Doctor. "Come in again Tuesday—Good morning!"

Then John Dolittle got a fine, big pair of green spectacles; and the plow horse stopped going blind in one eye and could see as well as ever.

And soon it became a common sight to see farm animals wearing glasses in the country round Puddleby; and a blind horse was a thing unknown.

And so it was with all the other animals that were brought to him. As soon as they found that he could talk their language, they told him where the pain was and how they felt, and of course it was easy for him to cure them.

Now all these animals went back and told their brothers and friends that there was a doctor in the little house with the big garden who really *was* a doctor. And whenever any creatures got sick—not only horses and cows and dogs—but all the little things of the fields, like harvest mice and water voles, badgers and bats, they came at once to his house on the edge of the town, so that his big garden was nearly always crowded with animals trying to get in to see him.

There were so many that came that he had to have special doors made for the different kinds. He wrote "HORSES" over the front door, "COWS" over the side door, and "SHEEP" on the kitchen door. Each kind of animal had a separate door—even the mice had a tiny tunnel made for them into the cellar, where they waited patiently in rows for the Doctor to come round to them.

And so, in a few years' time, every living thing for miles and miles got to know about John Dolittle, M.D. And the birds who flew to other countries in the winter told the animals in foreign lands of the wonderful doctor of Puddleby-on-the-Marsh, who could understand their talk and help them in their troubles. In this way he became famous among the animals—all over the world—better known even than he had been among the folks of the West Country. And he was happy and liked his life very much.

One afternoon when the Doctor was busy writing in a book, Polynesia sat in the window—as she nearly always did—looking out at the leaves blowing about in the garden. Presently she laughed aloud.

"What is it, Polynesia?" asked the Doctor, looking up from his book.

"I was just thinking," said the parrot; and she went on looking at the leaves.

"What were you thinking?"

"I was thinking about people," said Polynesia. "People make me sick. They think they're so wonderful. The world has been going on now for thousands of years, hasn't it? And the only thing in animal language that *people* have learned to understand is that when a dog wags his tail he means 'I'm glad!'—It's funny, isn't it? You are the very first man to talk like us. Oh, sometimes people annoy me dreadfully—such airs they put on—talking about 'the dumb animals.' *Dumb!*—Huh! Why I knew a macaw once who could say 'Good morning!' in seven different ways without once opening his mouth. He could talk every language—and Greek. An old professor with a gray beard bought him. But he didn't stay. He said the old man didn't talk Greek right, and he couldn't stand listening to him teach the language wrong. I often wonder what's become of him. That bird knew more geography than people will ever know. *People,* Golly! I suppose if people ever learn to fly—like any common hedge sparrow—we shall never hear the end of it!"

"You're a wise old bird," said the Doctor. "How old are you really? I know that parrots and elephants sometimes live to be very, very old."

"I can never be quite sure of my age," said Polynesia. "It's either a hundred and eighty-three or a hundred and eighty-two. But I know that when I first came here from Africa, King Charles was still hiding in the oak tree—because I saw him. He looked scared to death."

The Third Chapter

More Money Troubles

And soon now the Doctor began to make money again; and his sister, Sarah, bought a new dress and was happy.

Some of the animals who came to see him were so sick that they had to stay at the Doctor's house for a week. And when they were getting better they used to sit on chairs on the lawn.

And often even after they got well, they did not want to go away—they liked the Doctor and his house so much. And he never had the heart to refuse them when they asked if they could stay with him. So in this way he went on getting more and more pets.

Once when he was sitting on his garden wall, smoking a pipe in the evening, an Italian organ-grinder came round with a monkey on a string. The Doctor saw at once that the monkey's collar was too tight and that he was dirty and unhappy. So he took the monkey away from the Italian, gave the man a shilling, and told him to go. The organ-grinder got awfully angry and said that he wanted to keep the monkey. But the Doctor told him that if he didn't go away he would punch him on the nose. John Dolittle was a strong man, though he wasn't very tall. So the Italian went away saying rude things and the monkey stayed with Doctor Dolittle and had a good home. The other animals in the house called him "Chee-Chee"—which is a common word in monkey language, meaning "ginger."

And another time, when the circus came to Puddleby, the crocodile who had a bad toothache escaped at night and came into the Doctor's garden. The Doctor talked to him in crocodile language and took him into the house and made his tooth better. But when the crocodile saw what a nice house it was—with all the different places for the different kinds of animals—he too wanted to live with the Doctor. He asked couldn't he sleep in the fish pond at the bottom of the garden, if he promised not to eat the fish. When the circus men came to take him back he got so wild and savage that he frightened them away. But to everyone in the house he was always gentle as a kitten.

But now the old ladies grew afraid to send their lapdogs to Doctor Dolittle because of the crocodile; and the farmers wouldn't believe that he would not eat the lambs and sick calves they brought to be cured. So the Doctor went to the crocodile and told him he must go back to his circus. But he wept such big tears, and begged so hard to be allowed to stay, that the Doctor hadn't the heart to turn him out.

So then the Doctor's sister came to him and said,

"John, you must send that creature away. Now the farmers and the old ladies are afraid to send their animals to you—just as we were beginning to be well off again. Now we shall be ruined entirely. This is the last straw. I will no longer be housekeeper for you if you don't send away that alligator."

"It isn't an alligator," said the Doctor—"it's a crocodile."

"I don't care what you call it," said his sister. "It's a nasty thing to find under the bed. I won't have it in the house."

"But he has promised me," the Doctor answered, "that he will not bite anyone. He doesn't like the circus; and I haven't the money to send him back to Africa where he comes from. He minds his own business and on the whole is very well behaved. Don't be so fussy."

"I tell you I *will not* have him around," said Sarah. "He eats the linoleum. If you don't send him away this minute I'll—I'll go and get married!"

"All right," said the Doctor, "go and get married. It can't be helped." And he took down his hat and went out into the garden.

So Sarah Dolittle packed up her things and went off; and the Doctor was left all alone with his animal family.

And very soon he was poorer than he had ever been before. With all these mouths to fill, and the house to look after, and no one to do the mending, and no money coming in to pay the butcher's bill, things began to look very difficult. But the Doctor didn't worry at all.

"Money is a nuisance," he used to say. "We'd all be much better off if it had never been invented. What does money matter, so long as we are happy?"

But soon the animals themselves began to get worried. And one evening when the Doctor was asleep in his chair before the kitchen fire they began talking it over among themselves in whispers. And the owl, Too-Too, who was good at arithmetic, figured it out that there was only money enough left to last another week—if they each had one meal a day and no more.

Then the parrot said, "I think we all ought to do the housework ourselves. At least we can do that much. After all, it is for our sakes that the old man finds himself so lonely and so poor."

So it was agreed that the monkey, Chee-Chee, was to do the cooking and the mending; the dog was to sweep the floors; the duck was to dust and make the beds; the owl, Too-Too, was to keep the accounts; and the pig was to do the gardening. They made Polynesia, the parrot, housekeeper and laundress, because she was the oldest.

Of course at first they all found their new jobs very hard to do—all except Chee-Chee, who had hands and could do things like a man. But they soon got used to it; and they used to think it great fun to watch Jip, the dog, sweeping his tail over the floor with a rag tied onto it for a broom. After a little they got to do the work so well that the Doctor said that he had never had his house kept so tidy or so clean before.

In this way things went along all right for a while; but without money they found it very hard.

Then the animals made a vegetable and flower stall outside the garden gate and sold radishes and roses to the people that passed by along the road.

But still they didn't seem to make enough money to pay all the bills—and still the Doctor wouldn't worry. When the parrot came to him and told him that the fishmonger wouldn't give them any more fish, he said,

"Never mind. So long as the hens lay eggs and the cow gives milk we can have omelettes and junket. And there are plenty of vegetables left in the garden. The Winter is still a long way off. Don't fuss. That was the trouble with Sarah—she would fuss. I wonder how Sarah's getting on—an excellent woman—in some ways—Well, well!"

But the snow came earlier than usual that year; and although the old lame horse hauled in plenty of wood from the forest outside the town so they could have a big fire in the kitchen, most of the vegetables in the garden were gone, and the rest were covered with snow; and many of the animals were really hungry.

The Fourth Chapter

A Message from Africa

That Winter was a very cold one. And one night in December, when they were all sitting round the warm fire in the kitchen, and the Doctor was reading aloud to them out of books he had written himself in animal language, the owl, Too-Too, suddenly said,

"Sh! What's that noise outside?"

They all listened; and presently they heard the sound of someone running. Then the door flew open and the monkey, Chee-Chee, ran in, badly out of breath.

"Doctor!" he cried, "I've just had a message from a cousin of mine in Africa. There is a terrible sickness among the monkeys out there. They are all catching it—and they are dying in hundreds. They have heard of you, and beg you to come to Africa to stop the sickness."

"Who brought the message?" asked the Doctor, taking off his spectacles and laying down his book.

"A swallow," said Chee-Chee. "She is outside on the rain-butt."

"Bring her in by the fire," said the Doctor. "She must be perished with the cold. The swallows flew South six weeks ago!"

So the swallow was brought in, all huddled and shivering; and although she was a little afraid at first, she soon got warmed up and sat on the edge of the mantelpiece and began to talk.

When she had finished the Doctor said,

"I would gladly go to Africa—especially in this bitter weather. But I'm afraid we haven't money enough to buy the tickets. Get me the money-box, Chee-Chee."

So the monkey climbed up and got it off the top shelf of the dresser.

There was nothing in it—not one single penny!

"I felt sure there was twopence left," said the Doctor.

"There *was,*" said the owl. "But you spent it on a rattle for that badger's baby when he was teething."

"Did I?" said the Doctor. "Dear me, dear me! What a nuisance money is, to be sure! Well, never mind.

Perhaps if I go down to the seaside I shall be able to borrow a boat that will take us to Africa. I knew a seaman once who brought his baby to me with measles. Maybe he'll lend us his boat—the baby got well."

So early the next morning the Doctor went down to the seashore. And when he came back he told the animals it was all right—the sailor was going to lend them the boat.

Then the crocodile and the monkey and the parrot were very glad and began to sing, because they were going back to Africa, their real home. And the Doctor said,

"I shall only be able to take you three—with Jip the dog, Dab-Dab the duck, Gub-Gub the pig, and the owl, Too-Too. The rest of the animals, like the dormice and the water voles and the bats, they will have to go back and live in the fields where they were born till we come home again. But as most of them sleep through the Winter, they won't mind that—and besides, it wouldn't be good for them to go to Africa."

So then the parrot, who had been on long sea voyages before, began telling the Doctor all the things he would have to take with him on the ship.

"You must have plenty of pilot bread," she said—" 'hardtack' they call it. And you must have beef in cans—and an anchor."

"I expect the ship will have its own anchor," said the Doctor.

"Well, make sure," said Polynesia. "Because it's very important. You can't stop if you haven't got an anchor. And you'll need a bell."

"What's that for?" asked the Doctor.

"To tell the time by," said the parrot. "You go and ring it every half hour and then you know what time it is. And bring a whole lot of rope—it always comes in handy on voyages."

Then they began to wonder where they were going to get the money from to buy all the things they needed.

"Oh, bother it! Money again," cried the Doctor. "Goodness! I shall be glad to get to Africa where we don't have to have any! I'll go and ask the grocer if he will wait for his money till I get back—No, I'll send the sailor to ask him."

So the sailor went to see the grocer. And presently he came back with all the things they wanted.

Then the animals packed up; and after they had turned off the water so the pipes wouldn't freeze, and put up the shutters, they closed the house and gave the key to the old horse who lived in the stable. And when they had seen that there was plenty of hay in the loft to last the horse through the Winter, they carried all their luggage down to the seashore and got on to the boat.

The Cat's-meat-Man was there to see them off; and he brought a large suet pudding as a present for the Doctor because, he said he had been told, you couldn't get suet puddings in foreign parts.

As soon as they were on the ship, Gub-Gub, the pig, asked where the beds were, for it was four o'clock in the afternoon and he wanted his nap. So Polynesia took him downstairs into the inside of the ship and showed him the beds, set all on top of one another like bookshelves against a wall.

"Why, that isn't a bed!" cried Gub-Gub. "That's a shelf!"

"Beds are always like that on ships," said the parrot. "It isn't a shelf. Climb up into it and go to sleep. That's what you call 'a bunk.'"

"I don't think I'll go to bed yet," said Gub-Gub. "I'm too excited. I want to go upstairs again and see them start."

"Well, this is your first trip," said Polynesia. "You will get used to the life after a while." And she went back up the stairs of the ship, humming this song to herself:

> I've seen the Black Sea and the Red Sea;
>   I rounded the Isle of Wight;
> I discovered the Yellow River,
>   And the Orange too—by night.
> Now Greenland drops behind again,
>   And I sail the ocean Blue.
> I'm tired of all these colors, Jane,
>   So I'm coming back to you.

They were just going to start on their journey, when the Doctor said he would have to go back and ask the sailor the way to Africa.

But the swallow said she had been to that country many times and would show them how to get there.

So the Doctor told Chee-Chee to pull up the anchor and the voyage began.

The Fifth Chapter

The Great Journey

Now for six whole weeks they went sailing on and on, over the rolling sea, following the swallow who flew before the ship to show them the way. At night she

78

carried a tiny lantern, so they should not miss her in the dark; and the people on the other ships that passed said that the light must be a shooting star.

As they sailed further and further into the South, it got warmer and warmer. Polynesia, Chee-Chee, and the crocodile enjoyed the hot sun no end. They ran about laughing and looking over the side of the ship to see if they could see Africa yet.

But the pig and the dog and the owl, Too-Too, could do nothing in such weather, but sat at the end of the ship in the shade of a big barrel, with their tongues hanging out, drinking lemonade.

Dab-Dab, the duck, used to keep herself cool by jumping into the sea and swimming behind the ship. And every once in a while, when the top of her head got too hot, she would dive under the ship and come up on the other side. In this way, too, she used to catch herrings on Tuesdays and Fridays—when everybody on the boat ate fish to make the beef last longer.

When they got near to the Equator they saw some flying fishes coming towards them. And the fishes asked the parrot if this was Doctor Dolittle's ship. When she told them it was, they said they were glad, because the monkeys in Africa were getting worried that he would never come. Polynesia asked them how many miles they had yet to go; and the flying fishes said it was only fifty-five miles now to the coast of Africa.

And another time a whole school of porpoises came dancing through the waves; and they too asked Polynesia if this was the ship of the famous doctor. And when they heard that it was, they asked the parrot if the Doctor wanted anything for his journey.

And Polynesia said, "Yes. We have run short of onions."

"There is an island not far from here," said the porpoises, "where the wild onions grow tall and strong. Keep straight on—we will get some and catch up to you."

So the porpoises dashed away through the sea. And very soon the parrot saw them again, coming up behind, dragging the onions through the waves in big nets made of seaweed.

The next evening, as the sun was going down, the Doctor said,

"Get me the telescope, Chee-Chee. Our journey is nearly ended. Very soon we should be able to see the shores of Africa."

And about half an hour later, sure enough, they thought they could see something in front that might be land. But it began to get darker and darker and they couldn't be sure.

Then a great storm came up, with thunder and lightning. The wind howled, the rain came down in torrents, and the waves got so high they splashed right over the boat.

Presently there was a big BANG! The ship stopped and rolled over on its side.

"What's happened?" asked the Doctor, coming up from downstairs.

"I'm not sure," said the parrot, "but I think we're shipwrecked. Tell the duck to get out and see."

So Dab-Dab dived right down under the waves. And when she came up she said they had struck a rock; there was a big hole in the bottom of the ship; the water was coming in; and they were sinking fast.

"We must have run into Africa," said the Doctor. "Dear me, dear me!—Well—we must all swim to land."

But Chee-Chee and Gub-Gub did not know how to swim.

"Get the rope!" said Polynesia. "I told you it would come in handy. Where's that duck? Come here, Dab-Dab. Take this end of the rope, fly to the shore, and tie it on to a palm tree; and we'll hold the other end on the ship here. Then those that can't swim must climb along the rope till they reach the land. That's what you call a 'lifeline.'"

So they all got safely to the shore—some swimming, some flying; and those that climbed along the rope brought the Doctor's trunk and handbag with them.

But the ship was no good anymore—with the big hole in the bottom; and presently the rough sea beat it to pieces on the rocks and the timbers floated away.

Then they all took shelter in a nice dry cave they found, high up in the cliffs, till the storm was over.

When the sun came out next morning they went down to the sandy beach to dry themselves.

"Dear old Africa!" sighed Polynesia. "It's good to get back. Just think—it'll be a hundred and sixty-nine years tomorrow since I was here! And it hasn't changed a bit! Same old palm trees; same old red earth; same old black ants! There's no place like home!"

And the others noticed she had tears in her eyes—she was so pleased to see her country once again.

Then the Doctor missed his high hat; for it had been blown into the sea during the storm. So Dab-Dab went out to look for it. And presently she saw it, a long way off, floating on the water like a toy boat.

When she flew down to get it, she found one of the white mice, very frightened, sitting inside it.

"What are you doing here?" asked the duck. "You were told to stay behind in Puddleby."

"I didn't want to be left behind," said the mouse. "I wanted to see what Africa was like—I have relatives there. So I hid in the baggage and was brought on to the ship with the hardtack. When the ship sank I was terribly frightened—because I cannot swim far. I swam as long as I could, but I soon got all exhausted and thought I was going to sink. And then, just at that moment, the old man's hat came floating by; and I got into it because I did not want to be drowned."

So the duck took up the hat with the mouse in it and brought it to the Doctor on the shore. And they all gathered round to have a look.

"That's what you call a 'stowaway,' " said the parrot.

Presently, when they were looking for a place in the trunk where the white mouse could travel comfortably, the monkey, Chee-Chee, suddenly said,

"Sh! I hear footsteps in the jungle!"

They all stopped talking and listened. And soon a black man came down out of the woods and asked them what they were doing there.

"My name is John Dolittle—M.D.," said the Doctor. "I have been asked to come to Africa to cure the monkeys who are sick."

"You must all come before the King," said the black man.

"What king?" asked the Doctor, who didn't want to waste any time.

"The King of the Jolliginki," the man answered. "All

these lands belong to him; and all strangers must be brought before him. Follow me."

So they gathered up their baggage and went off, following the man through the jungle.

The Sixth Chapter

Polynesia and the King

When they had gone a little way through the thick forest they came to a wide, clear space; and they saw the King's palace, which was made of mud.

This was where the King lived with his Queen, Ermintrude, and their son, Prince Bumpo. The Prince was away fishing for salmon in the river. But the King and Queen were sitting under an umbrella before the palace door. And Queen Ermintrude was asleep.

When the Doctor had come up to the palace the King asked him his business; and the Doctor told him why he had come to Africa.

"You may not travel through my lands," said the King. "Many years ago a white man came to these shores, and I was very kind to him. But after he had dug holes in the ground to get the gold, and killed all the elephants to get their ivory tusks, he went away secretly in his ship—without so much as saying 'Thank you.' Never again shall a white man travel through the lands of Jolliginki."

Then the King turned to some of the black men who were standing near and said, "Take away this medicine man—with all his animals, and lock them up in my strongest prison."

So six of the black men led the Doctor and all his

pets away and shut them up in a stone dungeon. The dungeon had only one little window, high up in the wall, with bars in it; and the door was strong and thick.

Then they all grew very sad; and Gub-Gub, the pig, began to cry. But Chee-Chee said he would spank him if he didn't stop that horrible noise; and he kept quiet.

"Are we all here?" asked the Doctor, after he had got used to the dim light.

"Yes, I think so," said the duck and started to count them.

"Where's Polynesia?" asked the crocodile. "She isn't here."

"Are you sure?" said the Doctor. "Look again. Polynesia! Polynesia! Where are you?"

"I suppose she escaped," grumbled the crocodile. "Well, that's just like her!—Sneaked off into the jungle as soon as her friends got into trouble."

"I'm not that kind of a bird," said the parrot, climbing out of the pocket in the tail of the Doctor's coat. "You see, I'm small enough to get through the bars of that window; and I was afraid they would put me in a cage instead. So while the King was busy talking, I hid in the Doctor's pocket—and here I am! That's what you call a 'ruse,' " she said, smoothing down her feathers with her beak.

"Good Gracious!" cried the Doctor. "You're lucky I didn't sit on you."

"Now listen," said Polynesia, "tonight, as soon as it gets dark, I am going to creep through the bars of that window and fly over to the palace. And then—you'll see—I'll soon find a way to make the King let us all out of prison."

"Oh, what can *you* do?" said Gub-Gub, turning up his nose and beginning to cry again. "You're only a bird!"

"Quite true," said the parrot. "But do not forget that although I am only a bird, *I can talk like a man*—and I know these people."

So that night, when the moon was shining through the palm trees and all the King's men were asleep, the parrot slipped out through the bars of the prison and flew across to the palace. The pantry window had been broken by a tennis ball the week before; and Polynesia popped in through the hole in the glass.

She heard Prince Bumpo snoring in his bedroom at the back of the palace. Then she tiptoed up the stairs till she came to the King's bedroom. She opened the door gently and peeped in.

The Queen was away at a dance that night at her cousin's; but the King was in bed fast asleep.

Polynesia crept in, very softly, and got under the bed.

Then she coughed—just the way Doctor Dolittle used to cough. Polynesia could mimic any one.

The King opened his eyes and said sleepily: "Is that you, Ermintrude?" (He thought it was the Queen come back from the dance.)

Then the parrot coughed again—loud, like a man. And the King sat up, wide awake, and said, "Who's that?"

"I am Doctor Dolittle," said the parrot—just the way the Doctor would have said it.

"What are you doing in my bedroom?" cried the King. "How dare you get out of prison! Where are you?—I don't see you."

But the parrot just laughed—a long, deep jolly laugh, like the Doctor's.

"Stop laughing and come here at once, so I can see you," said the King.

"Foolish King!" answered Polynesia. "Have you forgotten that you are talking to John Dolittle, M.D.— the most wonderful man on earth? Of course you cannot see me. I have made myself invisible. There is nothing I cannot do. Now listen: I have come here tonight to warn you. If you don't let me and my animals travel through your kingdom, I will make you and all your people sick like the monkeys. For I can make people well and I can make people ill—just by raising my little finger. Send your soldiers at once to open the dungeon door, or you shall have mumps before the morning sun has risen on the hills of Jolliginki."

Then the King began to tremble and was very much afraid.

"Doctor," he cried, "it shall be as you say. Do not raise your little finger, please!" And he jumped out of bed and ran to tell the soldiers to open the prison door.

As soon as he was gone, Polynesia crept downstairs and left the palace by the pantry window.

But the Queen, who was just letting herself in at the backdoor with a latchkey, saw the parrot getting out through the broken glass. And when the King came back to bed she told him what she had seen.

Then the King understood that he had been tricked, and he was dreadfully angry. He hurried back to the prison at once.

But he was too late. The door stood open. The dungeon was empty. The Doctor and all his animals were gone.

The Seventh Chapter
The Bridge of Apes

Queen Ermintrude had never in her life seen her husband so terrible as he got that night. He gnashed his teeth with rage. He called everybody a fool. He threw his toothbrush at the palace cat. He rushed round in his nightshirt and woke up all his army and sent them into the jungle to catch the Doctor. Then he made all his servants go too—his cooks and his gardeners and his barber and Prince Bumpo's tutor—even the Queen, who was tired from dancing in a pair of tight shoes, was packed off to help the soldiers in their search.

All this time the Doctor and his animals were running through the forest towards the Land of the Monkeys as fast as they could go.

Gub-Gub, with his short legs, soon got tired; and the Doctor had to carry him—which made it pretty hard when they had the trunk and the handbag with them as well.

The King of the Jolliginki thought it would be easy for his army to find them, because the Doctor was in a strange land and would not know his way. But he was wrong, because the monkey, Chee-Chee, knew all the paths through the jungle—better even than the King's men did. And he led the Doctor and his pets to the very thickest part of the forest—a place where no man had ever been before—and hid them all in a big hollow tree between high rocks.

"We had better wait here," said Chee-Chee, "till the soldiers have gone back to bed. Then we can go on into the Land of the Monkeys."

So there they stayed the whole night through.

They often heard the King's men searching and talking in the jungle round about. But they were quite safe, for no one knew of that hiding place but Chee-Chee—not even the other monkeys.

At last, when daylight began to come through the thick leaves overhead, they heard Queen Ermintrude saying in a very tired voice that it was no use looking any more—that they might as well go back and get some sleep.

As soon as the soldiers had all gone home, Chee-Chee brought the Doctor and his animals out of the hiding place and they set off for the Land of the Monkeys.

It was a long, long way; and they often got very tired—especially Gub-Gub. But when he cried they gave him milk out of the coconuts which he was very fond of.

They always had plenty to eat and drink; because Chee-Chee and Polynesia knew all the different kinds of fruits and vegetables that grow in the jungle, and where to find them—like dates and figs and ground-nuts and ginger and yams. They used to make their lemonade out of the juice of wild oranges, sweetened with honey which they got from the bees' nests in hollow trees. No matter what it was they asked for, Chee-Chee and Polynesia always seemed to be able to get it for them— or something like it. They even got the Doctor some tobacco one day, when he had finished what he had brought with him and wanted to smoke.

At night they slept in tents made of palm leaves, on thick, soft beds of dried grass. And after a while they got used to walking such a lot and did not get so tired and enjoyed the life of travel very much.

But they were always glad when the night came and they stopped for their resting time. Then the Doctor used to make a little fire of sticks; and after they had had their supper, they would sit round in a ring, listening to Polynesia singing songs about the sea or to Chee-Chee telling stories of the jungle.

And many of the tales that Chee-Chee told were very interesting. Because although the monkeys had no history books of their own before Doctor Dolittle came to write them for them, they remember everything that happens by telling stories to their children. And Chee-Chee spoke of many things his grandmother had told him—tales of long, long, long ago, before Noah and the Flood—of the days when men dressed in bear skins and lived in holes in the rock and ate their mutton raw, because they did not know what cooking was—having never seen a fire. And he told them of the Great Mammoths and Lizards, as long as a train, that wandered over the mountains in those times, nibbling from the tree tops. And often they got so interested listening, that when he had finished they found their fire had gone right out; and they had to scurry round to get more sticks and build a new one.

Now when the King's army had gone back and told the King that they couldn't find the Doctor, the King sent them out again and told them that they must stay in the jungle till they caught him. So all this time, while the Doctor and his animals were going along towards the Land of the Monkeys, thinking themselves quite safe, they were still being followed by the King's men. If Chee-Chee had known this, he would most likely have hidden them again. But he didn't know it.

89

One day Chee-Chee climbed up a high rock and looked out over the treetops. And when he came down he said they were now quite close to the Land of the Monkeys and would soon be there.

And that same evening, sure enough, they saw Chee-Chee's cousin and a lot of other monkeys, who had not yet got sick, sitting in the trees by the edge of a swamp, looking and waiting for them. And when they saw the famous doctor really come, these monkeys made a tremendous noise, cheering and waving leaves and swinging out of the branches to greet him.

They wanted to carry his bag and his trunk and everything he had—and one of the bigger ones even carried Gub-Gub who had got tired again. Then two of them rushed on in front to tell the sick monkeys that the great doctor had come at last.

But the King's men, who were still following, had heard the noise of the monkeys cheering; and they at last knew where the Doctor was, and hastened on to catch him.

The big monkey carrying Gub-Gub was coming along behind slowly, and he saw the Captain of the army sneaking through the trees. So he hurried after the Doctor and told him to run.

Then they all ran harder than they had ever run in their lives; and the King's men, coming after them, began to run too; and the Captain ran hardest of all.

Then the Doctor tripped over his medicine bag and fell down in the mud, and the Captain thought he would surely catch him this time.

But the Captain had very long ears—though his hair was very short. And as he sprang forward to take hold of the Doctor, one of his ears caught fast in a tree; and the rest of the army had to stop and help him.

By this time the Doctor had picked himself up, and on they went again, running and running. And Chee-Chee shouted,

"It's all right! We haven't far to go now!"

But before they could get into the Land of the Monkeys, they came to a steep cliff with a river flowing below. This was the end of the Kingdom of Jolliginki; and the Land of the Monkeys was on the other side—across the river.

And Jip, the dog, looked down over the edge of the steep, steep cliff and said,

"Golly! How are we ever going to get across?"

"Oh, dear!" said Gub-Gub. "The King's men are quite close now—Look at them! I am afraid we are going to be taken back to prison again." And he began to weep.

But the big monkey who was carrying the pig dropped him on the ground and cried out to the other monkeys,

"Boys—a bridge! Quick!—Make a bridge! We've only a minute to do it. They've got the Captain loose, and he's coming on like a deer. Get lively! A bridge! A bridge!"

The Doctor began to wonder what they were going to make a bridge out of, and he gazed around to see if they had any boards hidden anyplace.

But when he looked back at the cliff, there, hanging across the river, was a bridge all ready for him—made of living monkeys! For while his back was turned, the monkeys—quick as a flash—had made themselves into a bridge, just by holding hands and feet.

And the big one shouted to the Doctor, "Walk over! Walk over—all of you—hurry!"

Gub-Gub was a bit scared, walking on such a narrow bridge at that dizzy height above the river. But he got over all right; and so did all of them.

John Dolittle was the last to cross. And just as he was getting to the other side, the King's men came rushing up to the edge of the cliff.

Then they shook their fists and yelled with rage. For they saw they were too late. The Doctor and all his animals were safe in the Land of the Monkeys and the bridge was pulled across to the other side.

Then Chee-Chee turned to the Doctor and said,

"Many great explorers and gray-bearded naturalists have lain long weeks hidden in the jungle waiting to see the monkeys do that trick. But we never let a white man get a glimpse of it before. You are the first to see the famous 'Bridge of Apes.'"

And the Doctor felt very pleased.

The Eighth Chapter

The Leader of the Lions

John Dolittle now became dreadfully, awfully busy. He found hundreds and thousands of monkeys sick— gorillas, orangutans, chimpanzees, dog-faced baboons, marmosettes, gray monkeys, red ones—all kinds. And many had died.

The first thing he did was to separate the sick ones from the well ones. Then he got Chee-Chee and his cousin to build him a little house of grass. The next thing: he made all the monkeys who were still well come and be vaccinated.

And for three days and three nights the monkeys kept coming from the jungles and the valleys and the hills to the little house of grass, where the Doctor sat all day and all night, vaccinating and vaccinating.

Then he had another house made—a big one, with a lot of beds in it; and he put all the sick ones in this house.

But so many were sick, there were not enough well ones to do the nursing. So he sent messages to the other animals, like the lions and the leopards and the antelopes, to come and help with the nursing.

But the Leader of the Lions was a very proud creature. And when he came to the Doctor's big house full of beds he seemed angry and scornful.

"Do you dare to ask me, Sir?" he said, glaring at the Doctor. "Do you dare to ask me—*ME, the King of Beasts,* to wait on a lot of dirty monkeys? Why, I wouldn't even eat them between meals!"

Although the lion looked very terrible, the Doctor tried hard not to seem afraid of him.

"I didn't ask you to eat them," he said quietly. "And besides, they're not dirty. They've all had a bath this morning. *Your* coat looks as though it needed brushing—badly. Now listen, and I'll tell you something: the day may come when the lions get sick. And if you don't help the other animals now, the lions may find themselves left all alone when *they* are in trouble. That often happens to proud people."

"The lions are never *in* trouble—they only *make* trouble," said the Leader, turning up his nose. And he stalked away into the jungle, feeling he had been rather smart and clever.

Then the leopards got proud too and said they wouldn't help. And then of course the antelopes—although they were too shy and timid to be rude to the Doctor like the lion—*they* pawed the ground, and smiled foolishly, and said they had never been nurses before.

And now the poor Doctor was worried frantic, wondering where he could get help enough to take care of all these thousands of monkeys in bed.

But the Leader of the Lions, when he got back to his den, saw his wife, the Queen Lioness, come running out to meet him with her hair untidy.

"One of the cubs won't eat," she said. "I don't know *what* to do with him. He hasn't taken a thing since last night."

And she began to cry and shake with nervousness—for she was a good mother, even though she was a lioness.

So the Leader went into his den and looked at his children—two very cunning little cubs, lying on the floor. And one of them seemed quite poorly.

Then the lion told his wife, quite proudly, just what he had said to the Doctor. And she got so angry she nearly drove him out of the den.

"You never *did* have a grain of sense!" she screamed. "All the animals from here to the Indian Ocean are talking about this wonderful man, and how he can cure any kind of sickness, and how kind he is—the only man in the whole world who can talk the language of the animals! And now, *now*—when we have a sick baby on our hands, you must go and offend him! You great booby! Nobody but a fool is ever rude to a *good* doctor. You—," and she started pulling her husband's hair.

94

"Go back to that white man at once," she yelled, "and tell him you're sorry. And take all the other empty-headed lions with you—and those stupid leopards and antelopes. Then do everything the Doctor tells you. Work hard! And perhaps he will be kind enough to come and see the cub later. Now be off!— *Hurry,* I tell you! You're not fit to be a father!"

And she went into the den next door, where another mother lion lived, and told her all about it.

So the Leader of the Lions went back to the Doctor and said, "I happened to be passing this way and thought I'd look in. Got any help yet?"

"No," said the Doctor. "I haven't. And I'm dreadfully worried."

"Help's pretty hard to get these days," said the lion. "Animals don't seem to want to work any more. You can't blame them—in a way. . . . Well, seeing you're in difficulties, I don't mind doing what I can—just to oblige you—so long as I don't have to wash the creatures. And I have told all the other hunting animals to come and do their share. The leopards should be here any minute now. . . . Oh, and by the way, we've got a sick cub at home. I don't think there's much the matter with him myself. But the wife is anxious. If you are around that way this evening, you might take a look at him, will you?"

Then the Doctor was very happy; for all the lions and the leopards and the antelopes and giraffes and zebras—all the animals of the forests and the mountains and the plains—came to help him in his work. There were so many of them that he had to send some away, and only keep the cleverest.

And now very soon the monkeys began to get better. At the end of a week the big house full of beds was half empty. And at the end of the second week the last monkey had got well.

Then the Doctor's work was done; and he was so tired he went to bed and slept for three days without even turning over.

The Ninth Chapter

The Monkeys' Council

Chee-Chee stood outside the Doctor's door, keeping everybody away till he woke up. Then John Dolittle told the monkeys that he must now go back to Puddleby.

They were very surprised at this; for they had thought that he was going to stay with them forever. And that night all the monkeys got together in the jungle to talk it over.

And the Chief Chimpanzee rose up and said,

"Why is it the good man is going away? Is he not happy here with us?"

But none of them could answer him.

Then the Grand Gorilla got up and said,

"I think we all should go to him and ask him to stay. Perhaps if we make him a new house and a bigger bed, and promise him plenty of monkey-servants to work for him and to make life pleasant for him—perhaps then he will not wish to go."

Then Chee-Chee got up; and all the others whispered, "Sh! Look! Chee-Chee, the great Traveler, is about to speak!"

And Chee-Chee said to the other monkeys,

"My friends, I am afraid it is useless to ask the Doctor to stay. He owes money in Puddleby; and he says he must go back and pay it."

And the monkeys asked him, "What is *money?*"

Then Chee-Chee told them that in the Land of the White Men you could get nothing without money; you could *do* nothing without money—that it was almost impossible to *live* without money.

And some of them asked, "But can you not even eat and drink without paying?"

But Chee-Chee shook his head. And then he told them that even he, when he was with the organ-grinder, had been made to ask the children for money.

And the Chief Chimpanzee turned to the Oldest Orangutan and said, "Cousin, surely these Men be strange creatures! Who would wish to live in such a land? My gracious, how paltry!"

Then Chee-Chee said,

"When we were coming to you we had no boat to cross the sea in and no money to buy food to eat on our journey. So a man lent us some biscuits; and we said we would pay him when we came back. And we borrowed a boat from a sailor; but it was broken on the rocks when we reached the shores of Africa. Now the Doctor says he must go back and get the sailor another boat—because the man was poor and his ship was all he had."

And the monkeys were all silent for a while, sitting quite still upon the ground and thinking hard.

At last the Biggest Baboon got up and said,

"I do not think we ought to let this good man leave our land till we have given him a fine present to take with him, so that he may know we are grateful for all that he has done for us."

And a little, tiny red monkey who was sitting up in a tree shouted down,

"I think that too!"

And then they all cried out, making a great noise, "Yes, yes. Let us give him the finest present a White Man ever had!"

Now they began to wonder and ask one another what would be the best thing to give him. And one said, "Fifty bags of cocoanuts!" And another—"A hundred bunches of bananas!—At least he shall not have to buy his fruit in the Land Where You Pay to Eat!"

But Chee-Chee told them that all these things would be too heavy to carry so far and would go bad before half was eaten.

"If you want to please him," he said, "give him an animal. You may be sure he will be kind to it. Give him some rare animal they have not got in the menageries."

And the monkeys asked him, "What are *menageries?*"

Then Chee-Chee explained to them that menageries were places in the Land of the White Men, where animals were put in cages for people to come and look at. And the monkeys were very shocked and said to one another,

"These Men are like thoughtless young ones—stupid and easily amused. Sh! It is a prison he means."

So then they asked Chee-Chee what rare animals it could be that they should give the Doctor—one the White Men had not seen before. And the Major of the Marmosettes asked,

"Have they an iguana over there?"

But Chee-Chee said, "Yes, there is one in the London Zoo."

And another asked, "Have they an okapi?"

But Chee-Chee said, "Yes. In Belgium, where my organ-grinder took me five years ago, they had an okapi in a big city they call Antwerp."

And another asked, "Have they a pushmi-pullyu?"

Then Chee-Chee said, "No. No White Man has ever seen a pushmi-pullyu. Let us give him that."

The Tenth Chapter

The Rarest Animal of All

Pushmi-pullyus are now extinct. That means, there aren't any more. But long ago, when Doctor Dolittle was alive, there were some of them still left in the deepest jungles of Africa; and even then they were very, very scarce. They had no tail, but a head at each end, and sharp horns on each head. They were very shy and terribly hard to catch. The black men get most of their animals by sneaking up behind them while they are not looking. But you could not do this with the pushmi-pullyu—because, no matter which way you came towards him, he was always facing you. And besides, only one half of him slept at a time. The other head was always awake—and watching. This was why they were never caught and never seen in Zoos. Though many of the greatest huntsmen and the cleverest menagerie-keepers spent years of their lives searching through the jungles in all weathers for pushmi-pullyus, not a single one had ever been caught. Even then, years ago, he was the only animal in the world with two heads.

Well, the monkeys set out hunting for this animal through the forest. And after they had gone a good many miles, one of them found peculiar footprints near the edge of a river; and they knew that a pushmi-pullyu must be very near that spot.

Then they went along the bank of the river a little way and they saw a place where the grass was high and thick; and they guessed that he was in there.

So they all joined hands and made a great circle round the high grass. The pushmi-pullyu heard them coming; and he tried hard to break through the ring of monkeys. But he couldn't do it. When he saw that it was no use trying to escape, he sat down and waited to see what they wanted.

They asked him if he would go with Doctor Dolittle and be put on show in the Land of the White Men.

But he shook both his heads hard and said, "Certainly not!"

They explained to him that he would not be shut up in a menagerie but would just be looked at. They told him that the Doctor was a very kind man but hadn't any money; and people would pay to see a two-headed animal and the Doctor would get rich and could pay for the boat he had borrowed to come to Africa in.

But he answered, "No. You know how shy I am—I hate being stared at." And he almost began to cry.

Then for three days they tried to persuade him.

And at the end of the third day he said he would come with them and see what kind of a man the Doctor was, first.

So the monkeys traveled back with the pushmi-pullyu. And when they came to where the Doctor's little house of grass was, they knocked on the door.

The duck, who was packing the trunk, said, "Come in!"

And Chee-Chee very proudly took the animal inside and showed him to the Doctor.

"What in the world is it?" asked John Dolittle, gazing at the strange creature.

"Lord save us!" cried the duck. "How does it make up its mind?"

"It doesn't look to me as though it had any," said Jip, the dog.

"This, Doctor," said Chee-Chee, "is the pushmi-pullyu—the rarest animal of the African jungles, the only two-headed beast in the world! Take him home with you and your fortune's made. People will pay any money to see him."

"But I don't want any money," said the Doctor.

"Yes, you do," said Dab-Dab, the duck. "Don't you remember how we had to pinch and scrape to pay the butcher's bill in Puddleby? And how are you going to get the sailor the new boat you spoke of—unless we have the money to buy it?"

"I was going to make him one," said the Doctor.

"Oh, do be sensible!" cried Dab-Dab. "Where would you get all the wood and the nails to make one with?— And besides, what are you going to live on? We shall be poorer than ever when we get back. Chee-Chee's perfectly right: take the funny-looking thing along, do!"

"Well, perhaps there is something in what you say," murmured the Doctor. "It certainly would make a nice new kind of pet. But does the er—what-do-you-call-it really want to go abroad?"

"Yes, I'll go," said the pushmi-pullyu who saw at once, from the Doctor's face, that he was a man to be trusted. "You have been so kind to the animals here—and the monkeys tell me that I am the only one who will do. But you must promise that if I do not like it in the Land of the White Men you will send me back."

"Why, certainly—of course, of course," said the Doctor. "Excuse me, surely you are related to the Deer Family, are you not?"

"Yes," said the pushmi-pullyu—"to the Abyssinian Gazelles and the Asiatic Chamois—on my mother's side. My father's great-grandfather was the last of the Unicorns."

"Most interesting!" murmured the Doctor; and he took a book out of the trunk which Dab-Dab was packing and began turning the pages. "Let us see if Buffon* says anything——"

"I notice," said the duck, "that you only talk with one of your mouths. Can't the other head talk as well?"

"Oh, yes," said the pushmi-pullyu. "But I keep the other mouth for eating—mostly. In that way I can talk while I am eating without being rude. Our people have always been very polite."

When the packing was finished and everything was ready to start, the monkeys gave a grand party for the Doctor, and all the animals of the jungle came. And they had pineapples and mangoes and honey and all sorts of good things to eat and drink.

After they had all finished eating, the Doctor got up and said,

---

* *Buffon.* A famous French natural historian.

"My friends: I am not clever at speaking long words after dinner, like some men; and I have just eaten many fruits and much honey. But I wish to tell you that I am very sad at leaving your beautiful country. Because I have things to do in the Land of the White Men, I must go. After I have gone, remember never to let the flies settle on your food before you eat it; and do not sleep on the ground when the rains are coming. I—er—er—I hope you will all live happily ever after."

When the Doctor stopped speaking and sat down, all the monkeys clapped their hands a long time and said to one another, "Let it be remembered always among our people that he sat and ate with us, here, under the trees. For surely he is the Greatest of Men!"

And the Grand Gorilla, who had the strength of seven horses in his hairy arms, rolled a great rock up to the head of the table and said,

"This stone for all time shall mark the spot."

And even to this day, in the heart of the jungle, that stone still is there. And monkey mothers, passing through the forest with their families, still point down at it from the branches and whisper to their children, "Sh! There it is—look—where the Good White Man sat and ate food with us in the Year of the Great Sickness!"

Then, when the party was over, the Doctor and his pets started out to go back to the seashore. And all the monkeys went with him as far as the edge of their country, carrying his trunk and bags to see him off.

The Last Chapter
Home Again

March winds had come and gone; April's showers were over; May's buds had opened into flower; and the June sun was shining on the pleasant fields, when John Dolittle at last got back to his own country.

But he did not yet go home to Puddleby. First he went traveling through the land with the pushmi-pullyu in a gypsy wagon, stopping at all the country fairs. And there, with the acrobats on one side of them and the Punch-and-Judy show on the other, they would hang out a big sign which read, "COME AND SEE THE MARVELOUS TWO-HEADED ANIMAL FROM THE JUNGLES OF AFRICA. Admission SIXPENCE."

And the pushmi-pullyu would stay inside the wagon, while the other animals would lie about underneath. The Doctor sat in a chair in front taking the sixpences and smiling on the people as they went in; and Dab-Dab was kept busy all the time scolding him because he would let the children in for nothing when she wasn't looking.

And menagerie-keepers and circus men came and asked the Doctor to sell them the strange creature, saying they would pay a tremendous lot of money for him. But the Doctor always shook his head and said,

"No. The pushmi-pullyu shall never be shut up in a cage. He shall be free always to come and go, like you and me."

Many curious sights and happenings they saw in this wandering life; but they all seemed quite ordinary after the great things they had seen and done in foreign lands. It was very interesting at first, being sort of part of a circus; but after a few weeks they all got dreadfully tired of it and the Doctor and all of them were longing to go home.

But so many people came flocking to the little wagon and paid the sixpence to go inside and see the pushmi-pullyu that very soon the Doctor was able to give up being a showman.

And one fine day, when the hollyhocks were in full bloom, he came back to Puddleby a rich man, to live in the little house with the big garden.

And the old lame horse in the stable was glad to see him; and so were the swallows who had already built their nests under the eaves of his roof and had young ones. And Dab-Dab was glad, too, to get back to the house she knew so well—although there was a terrible lot of dusting to be done, with cobwebs everywhere.

And after Jip had gone and shown his golden collar to the conceited collie next door, he came back and began running round the garden like a crazy thing, looking for the bones he had buried long ago, and chasing the rats out of the tool shed; while Gub-Gub dug up the horseradish, which had grown three feet high in the corner by the garden wall.

And the Doctor went and saw the sailor who had lent him the boat, and he bought two new ships for him and a rubber doll for his baby; and he paid the grocer for the food he had lent him for the journey to Africa. And he bought another piano and put the white mice back in it—because they said the bureau drawer was drafty.

Even when the Doctor had filled the old money-box on the dresser shelf, he still had a lot of money left; and he had to get three more money-boxes, just as big, to put the rest in.

"Money," he said, "is a terrible nuisance. But it's nice not to have to worry."

"Yes," said Dab-Dab, who was toasting muffins for his tea, "it is indeed!"

And when the Winter came again, and the snow flew against the kitchen window, the Doctor and his animals would sit round the big, warm fire after supper; and he would read aloud to them out of his books.

But far away in Africa, where the monkeys chattered in the palm trees before they went to bed under the big yellow moon, they would say to one another,

"I wonder what The Good Man's doing now—over there, in the Land of the White Men! Do you think he ever will come back?"

And Polynesia would squeak out from the vines,

"I think he will—I guess he will—I hope he will!"

And then the crocodile would grunt up at them from the black mud of the river,

"I'm SURE he will—Go to sleep!"